FIRST CASUALTY

FIRST CASUALTY

THE PSYCHIC GUARDIAN ANGEL™ BOOK ONE

A.W. POWERS

MARLOWE & VANE

DON'T MISS OUR NEW RELEASES

Join the Marlowe and Vane email list to be notified of new releases and special promotions (which happen often) by following this link:

https://marloweandvane.lmbpn.com/newsletter/

Published by Marlowe & Vane
an imprint of LMBPN Publishing
PMB 196, 2540 South Maryland Pkwy
Las Vegas, NV 89109

Version 1.00, June 2023
eBook ISBN: 979-8-88878-139-5
Print ISBN: 979-8-88878-434-1

THE FIRST CASUALTY TEAM

Thanks to our Beta Team:
John Ashmore, Kelly O'Donnell, Alison Kelly, Rachel
Beckford, Jan Hunnicutt

JIT Readers

Wendy L Bonell
Rachel Beckford
Jan Hunnicutt
John Ashmore

Editor
SkyFyre Editing Team

For my wife Jody, and my daughters Gillian and Lauren, who watched the process and believed as much as I did. You've been my love and my joy. I am blessed. Thank you.

CHAPTER ONE

Daniels, August 2000

Great Grandma Nan has been dead since my mother was a little girl, but that hadn't stopped her from visiting me every once in a while to deliver a cryptic message. She appeared in my dreams, maybe in my room, and we'd talk for a few minutes before she disappeared.

The first time she visited, Great Grandma Nan told me, "Jacob, pay attention to your feelings. But don't mind how others react."

I followed my feelings and led a woman and her son away from a Metro Transit bus stop seconds before a truck crashed through it. The second part of her message was intended to prepare me for the woman's reaction. After Mom told her I had guided us there, the woman was afraid of me.

Another time, Great Grandma Nan stated, "Listen with your heart."

I helped find a little kid who was separated from his

mom at the Minneapolis Farmers Market. I simply knew where he was and told Emily, a telepath I was having a psychic conversation with, where to look. Emily followed my directions and led the police to the boy. I watched as he was reunited with his relieved mother, who was unaware of how he had been found.

Then Great Grandma Nan came and remarked, "Hard times are coming. Be careful. You'll have to be strong."

After she left, I woke and could not fall back to sleep. I lay there and stared at the ceiling, then read for a while. The book may not have been the best choice. *Keeper of the Children* by William H. Hallahan. It included out-of-body experiences and murderous cats. Then I meditated.

It didn't work very well. I couldn't see, hear, or feel my breath, couldn't find focus. I may have fallen asleep, though, because I had a vision of myself being chased. Since I normally don't have visions, it had to have been a nightmare, which meant I had to have fallen asleep.

After that, I got out of bed. Yoga was better at getting me thinking about something else, namely, not falling. In spite of how good my balance is most days, it was a concern here. My mind would drift, and I'd begin to lean, which is the first step in falling out of a tree pose where I stood on one foot, the other foot off the floor and pressed against the knee holding me up.

I traveled back and forth across the living room, practicing the Tae Kwon Do routine my instructor Mr. Lee had taught me. He would be glad to hear I was doing exercises outside of class, but since I wasn't actually hitting something, I didn't feel any better.

When I knew he'd be awake, I called my friend John Thompson. He was willing to play some tennis, something we did on a regular basis. We would often play doubles, with John and our friend Warren Marsh playing against John's sister Rachel and me. John and I met at the courts near Loring Elementary. Most days, playing singles, we're about even. If I can consistently return his serve, I can sometimes win. This time he beat me badly. He jogged around the court, arms and racquet over his head as he chanted, "And the crowd goes wild. Thompson slaughters Daniels. Thompson slaughters Daniels."

As we walked away from the courts, John asked, "What's wrong with you today? You played like crap."

"Yeah, I know."

"I can't believe how many times I aced you," he commented. "I may beat you on quite a few serves, but usually, you take a whack at it and are pretty good at getting to the ball."

"Your serve was really good today," I told him.

"No, it wasn't. I hit a lot of them into the net, and you didn't even know it. Half of my aces came off my lame second serve. I probably could have used third or fourth serves and gotten away with it."

"There are no third or fourth serves," I pointed out.

"I know. But you stood there and watched the ball go by."

"Are you sure?"

"Yeah, I felt like I was playing alone."

"Didn't stop you from gloating when we finished," I noted.

"Of course not," John replied. "Opportunities to gloat are rare, so you have to take advantage of every chance you get. So what's your deal?"

"I don't know what's going on." I drew a deep breath. "I feel like I'm supposed to be somewhere but have no idea where, when, or why." We walked part of a block in silence. "Add that to nightmares and sleeping like crap and 'Thompson slaughters Daniels.'"

"And the crowd went wild," John added, his arms over his head.

John's mom pulled the family's Ford Taurus to the curb next to us. "Headed home?"

"We are," John confirmed. "Are you?"

"I wasn't supposed to work today," Mrs. Thompson noted. "But I went in for a while, made sure everything was organized for the new girl. Then I stopped at the grocery store. Now, I have the rest of the day off, so yeah, I'm on my way home. Get in."

We piled in, and John rode in front next to Mrs. Thompson. He chattered away about how Thompson had slaughtered Daniels. I kept my gaze locked out the window, hoping I might pick up a clue as to what I was supposed to be doing. Everything looked the same as it did most days. Yet the thought I was supposed to be somewhere doing something wouldn't go away.

Mrs. Thompson parked the car at the curb in front of the house and popped the trunk. We circled to the rear of the Taurus, and she loaded John's arms with her purchases. He gave me a dirty look as I walked up the sidewalk, unencumbered beyond our racquets and tennis balls. I smiled back. I've told him before that his mom likes me best.

We took the three steps onto the porch, and Mrs. Thompson pulled open the screen door. Her right hand slid the key into the lock, her left closed on the doorknob. She inhaled sharply and twitched a little taller. "Something's happened to Rachel."

CHAPTER TWO

Latisha & Hanley, March 1997

Latisha Ford watched the cop search for her. He followed a dirt path through the park on the other side of the fence. Until today, Latisha had used the path every day on her way to or from school. The park was a nice shortcut.

The cop's radio made a noise. His hand went to his shoulder, and Latisha heard a button click. "Hanley," the cop stated.

"Hey, Rich, we're striking out over here by the school," Latisha heard someone say through the radio. "Plus, it's getting dark. We're thinking we have to quit for the night, try something else."

Latisha stepped up to the fence. It was wrought iron, with a horizontal bar about a foot above the ground and another about seven feet up. There were half-inch wide, eight-foot vertical bars every six inches, close enough to keep some stupid kid from putting his head through and getting stuck. Latisha put her hands on a couple of the bars and leaned forward, pressing her head against them.

Hanley pressed the button again. "I'm still in the park. I've got my flashlight, so I'm going to keep looking. See if I can finish here."

"All right. Call if you need us," the voice from the radio noted. "Otherwise, have a good night."

"Yeah, you too." Hanley sighed and looked around. He took a few more steps along the path, then stepped to the side and got down on one knee. Latisha wondered what he found. He brushed at the grass, leaned closer, then looked around slowly. Still kneeling, he dug into the pocket of his uniform pants, came out with something, and set it on the ground. Latisha saw that it was a quarter. Hanley stood, pulled a small digital camera from his coat pocket, and took a few pictures of the ground and the quarter.

He walked a few steps further, bent, and studied the path. He set down another quarter and snapped more pictures. The coin glinted in the camera flash. He stepped away from the path and took pictures of the fence and trees.

Latisha stepped through the fence and walked to the cop. She waved her hand in front of his face, but he stepped through her, shivered like he had a sudden chill, and continued down the path. Latisha looked at the ground next to the quarter and saw a footprint in the dirt. When she lifted her foot and looked at the bottom of her boot, it matched the footprint.

She turned and followed the cop. Hanley continued down the path, then came to an abrupt stop. He leaned a bit, pulled out a flashlight, and shined it on the ground.

The light swept sideways, back and forth across the path and the grass on either side. He walked in a large circle, shining his light on the same place. He took more pictures, circled again, and lowered the camera.

Hanley pressed the button on his shoulder microphone. "Hey, Krause, you still there?"

"Sure am. What's up, Rich?"

"I may be onto something near the rear of the park, where it backs up to the cemetery."

"What do you see?"

"Footprints. Something that suggests a scuffle," Hanley remarked.

Latisha stepped up to Hanley, looked around and at the ground where his light was shining. This was the spot where the man had grabbed her. He was strong, and no matter how hard she fought, she couldn't get away. He was the kind of man her mom would describe as a Bad Man. Her mom tried to think the best of everyone and would not use strong language to describe somebody. Her father, however, would have called him Motherfucker.

Latisha's mom didn't like how much her dad swore. It made Latisha laugh, especially when he would tell her, "Don't let your momma hear you talking like that. I'd be in deep shit." Latisha thought of the man who grabbed her as the miserable bastard who had hit her, threatened her family, made it so she couldn't breathe, then hurt her bad. She'd heard the name "miserable bastard" in a movie she wasn't supposed to have seen. She wondered how she could hurt the bad man back.

Hanley's radio crackled. "Wait there. We're on our way."

"I can't. I've got to keep looking," Hanley replied. "I'll

leave my extra light standing on the path, shining up. I'm going to keep searching."

"Okay, we'll be there soon. Be careful."

"I'll do my best. Make it quick." Hanley pulled a smaller flashlight from a pocket on his pants leg, turned it on, and stood it in the grass outside the circle he had walked. He set another quarter on the ground and took more pictures.

"You can find me," Latisha remarked.

Hanley acted like he didn't hear her.

He took baby steps as he moved away from where his flashlight stood. "Okay, little girl," he mused. "You were here, and so was someone else." His gaze scanned the park. "He grabbed you. You put up a hell of a fight, but he dragged you away. So where are you now?"

"I'm right here," Latisha insisted. "Why can't you hear me?" She stomped her way to the flashlight and kicked at it hard.

The flashlight flew from where it sat and hit Hanley in the middle of the back.

"Oh, my God." Latisha's hands flew up and covered her mouth. She laughed, wide-eyed. "I didn't mean to do that."

"What the hell?" Hanley spun, his hand going to his gun. The beam of his large flashlight swept the area, stopped where he'd left the smaller light, and moved to where it landed. He picked up and examined the light, then stood it on the ground where it had been before taking flight. He scanned the surrounding area before he returned to following the scuff marks on the ground.

Latisha wanted to kick the flashlight again to see if she could make it fly one more time. But she wanted Officer

Hanley to find her soon. He might not if she kept kicking distractions his way.

Hanley followed the trail to where a hedge met the fence. He pushed back the branches and found an opening his six-foot-eight, two-hundred-and-eighty-pound frame might fit through. Someone smaller could have made it through the gap with no problem, even dragging a girl who was putting up a good fight.

Latisha ran to the fence and stepped through as Hanley forced his way through the gap. One of the branches scratched his cheek, and another tore the sleeve of his uniform coat. He didn't seem to notice.

He examined things that might be a trail. A bent piece of grass, a crinkled leaf, an impression in the dirt. Then he took a hunched step while the flashlight looked for the next sign to illuminate. Hanley was careful not to disturb anything that might be important. Things that could become evidence if need be.

She stood in front of him. "You're getting warmer."

Hanley stepped through her and shivered again. "What's with these cold spots?" he asked, his voice fading into the faltering light. The early evening was cool, becoming more so as the sun fell, but the cold spots cut through his coat and went to his bones.

"I know you can find me," Latisha told him.

He followed his flashlight to the next bit of trail sign. He stopped and shone the light around the cemetery. Few markers encompassed this area. It was reserved for future expansion, the upcoming dead. However, a paved road wound through this area of the cemetery toward a small

11

building, presumably used by the grounds crew to store tools and supplies.

"You're getting warmer," Latisha announced.

The trail led to the building. Hanley stepped to the side of the trail and walked to the rear of the building.

"Yep, warmer."

Behind the building was a pile of branches intended to become compost or mulch.

"Warmer."

Hanley pulled off the top layer of branches and set it to the side.

"You're getting hot now."

He lifted another layer.

"You're burning up."

He pulled off another branch and uncovered a boot with a bare leg extending away from it. The boot and the leg matched the one Latisha held out for him to see, though he still couldn't.

Hanley gently lifted the branches one at a time until he'd uncovered the dead body of Latisha Ford.

"Thank you," Latisha whispered.

If Hanley could have seen her next to him, he would have noticed her tears.

CHAPTER THREE

<u>Daniels, August 2000</u>

John Thompson described learning his mom had psychic ability as a major turning point in his short life. I assured him the most significant moment in his long life was when he met me. John called his mom's talent "tactile reception." I don't know if he read that somewhere or made it up, but I thought it sounded good. According to him, she would touch an object and receive a message about someone. The object was usually related to that person in some way. Like the doorknob to the family home.

I had never seen a demonstration of Mrs. Thompson's talent, but I knew as soon as she stated, "Something's happened to Rachel," that I was witnessing her ability in action, and I needed to find Rachel.

As a soon-to-be eighth grader, I should not have been so fixated on a girl that she became my reason for getting up in the morning, but I was with Rachel Thompson. The image of her smiling face, blue eyes flecked with gold, clear skin, and long legs entered my mind too often to track.

I had been looking at her face for years before I knew her. She had passed through many dreams. We never talked or touched, and she rarely smiled. Yet the first time I met her in person, I immediately recognized her as the girl in my dreams. And that was in spite of the experts insisting you couldn't dream about a face you had never seen in real life.

John and I met when we were in fifth grade, shortly after I changed schools. One afternoon, I followed my feelings and found him on his back on the floor with a bully punching him and another watching. They had been abusing John and a number of other kids for years. I left the bullies bloodied with a good idea of what would happen if they didn't let up on John and the others.

John had already heard about me and my ability to find things, like a teacher's dog, someone's textbooks, or another kid's bicycle. He'd decided I was a psychic he should know and had been searching for me. After I found and defended him, we became friends. Or he became mine, and I became his freakish research subject.

Rachel was three years older than us. Though I didn't spend time with many girls or look at them with a critical eye, I thought she was probably the most beautiful thing inhabiting my world or any other and appreciated every moment I got to be near her.

Fortunately, I spent a lot of time at John and Rachel's house. Mr. and Mrs. Thompson made me feel welcome and included me in a lot of their activities. Since my father died when I was four, I enjoyed hanging with and learning from Mr. Thompson. I spent more time with him than any other adult male besides Mr. Lee, my martial arts instructor.

Rachel was the real reason I looked forward to being included there, though. I was there the first time the family went sailing and the first time Rachel tried water-skiing. I was there when she cut her finger, and I rode along with the family so she could have it stitched. I was there after she had her broken leg set, waited on her as best as I could, assisted in her physical therapy, and taught her to play tennis. When I defended her from a boyfriend who wouldn't listen when she said no, she referred to me as her guardian angel. As far as I was concerned, I was her protector and always would be.

Tactile reception seemed to leave Mrs. Thompson frozen in place. I threw the racquets and balls into the nearest patio chair, stepped in close, pulled her hands off the knob, and finished unlocking the door. I swung the door open and raced inside. I was most of the way up to Rachel's second-floor bedroom when John mentioned, "She isn't here. She left before I did."

Rachel wasn't in her bedroom. The bathroom door was closed, but I barged in. It was empty. I passed nobody on my way to the basement.

John stood in the entryway; Mrs. Thompson was still outside the front door. She was pale and wobbly. I was headed for the garage but stopped in front of her. "Did you see something? Is that how your gift works?"

She shook her head. "No. I just know."

That was usually my line. I was the one who used my feelings to know things.

I continued on. No one was in the garage. Mr. Thompson's car was gone, and Mrs. Thompson's was in front of the house. Rachel's bike stood against the side wall, John's against the back. I came back to the porch, took Mrs. Thompson by the hand, and led her into the house. John was still in the entryway and stepped to the side as we came in.

"We have to find her," I declared.

"I know," John agreed. "But how? I have no idea where she was going or how early she left."

Mrs. Thompson seemed completely out of it, as if getting a message about her daughter had left her catatonic. I led her to the couch where I had prevented Rachel from being raped by her boyfriend. "Are you okay?" I asked.

"No," she whispered. "Something has happened to Rachel."

"When did she leave?" I asked. "Where was she going?"

Her eyelids fluttered, and she shook her head. A little color returned. "Rachel was meeting a group of friends at the Coffee Nook, and they were going shopping. They would drop her at work afterward. She doesn't have to be at the theater until five."

I glanced at my watch. It was almost eleven. "She didn't make it to the Coffee Nook."

"How do you know?" John asked.

"Funny feeling. I just know."

John stared at me. His slight twitch may have been nodding acceptance of what I knew.

Mrs. Thompson sagged back onto the couch, and a tear

dropped down her cheek. She gave no indication she was listening to us.

"Okay," John stated. "How do we prove it?"

"Would they have called or come looking for her if she didn't show?" I asked.

"I don't know," John claimed. "Some of her friends are flaky. They forget things, like each other, things they've agreed to do." He shook his head. "Sometimes Rachel wonders if they have ADHD, or might be stupid or just mean."

"Sound like great friends," I commented. "Remind me to find some exactly like them some day."

"For sure," John declared. "But maybe one of them remembered to call. We should check the answering machine."

The phone sat on the sofa behind Mrs. Thompson. It didn't include an answering machine. "I didn't know you had one."

"It's in the kitchen." He led the way.

The kitchen phone was a light blue Thinline hanging on the wall between the basement door and the built-in hutch. It did not include an answering machine either. John opened the door to the hutch. Sitting on a shelf was a machine with a cord that extended up to the phone. "I didn't know that was there," I noted. "I've never had a call go to a machine, and I've never seen you check it."

"I don't," John confirmed. "No one leaves me messages. You only call when you know I'm home."

The message indicator light blinked. John punched the button, and the machine told us we had one message.

Mrs. Thompson wandered into the kitchen as it began

to play. She stood behind John and stared at the machine. "Rachel, it's Angelica. It's almost ten. We're about to leave the Coffee Nook, and you're over an hour late already. You better have a really cute excuse for missing this. After all, it was your idea."

John's finger went to the delete button.

"Don't." I grabbed his arm. "It might be important."

"How?" he asked.

"I have no idea. I just think it might be."

He pulled his hand away from the machine. "You were right," he remarked. "She didn't make it to the Coffee Nook."

Mrs. Thompson drifted out of the kitchen. She went up the stairs, and we heard the door to Rachel's room close.

"Should we start looking for her?" I asked.

"Where?"

"Between here and the Coffee Nook."

"That's a lot of ground to cover," John remarked. "We don't even know which way she went."

"No, but maybe we'll see something, and everything will click, or I'll get a funny feeling and know which way to go."

"That's a huge maybe."

"What else are we going to do?" I asked.

"My dad always tells me, 'If you're not sure what to do in a crisis situation, wait for adult supervision.'" John's voice climbed in pitch. It was as close to a whine as I'd ever heard from him.

"Your dad is smart and has lots of ideas I like, but I'm not sure I agree this time."

"But..."

"Think about it," I suggested. "We have adult supervision right now. Except the knowledge that something happened has left her pretty much out of it."

"And if we go searching and Rachel comes home, no one will know where we are," John stated. "They'll have to worry about us instead."

"Yeah, but nobody said anything would happen to us. Only Rachel," I declared. "Maybe we can find her."

"There's got to be something else we can do."

"Tell you what. I'll take your bike, cover a little ground, come back in, say…" I looked at my watch. "An hour." I nodded, and John stared at me. "I have to do something," I told him. "You stay here, take care of your mom, and listen for the phone. That way, we have everything covered until Rachel comes back. I can look a little, and I won't be gone longer than planned. Or else I'll find a way to call."

"I don't like it," John noted. "But at least we're doing something."

A family portrait hung on their refrigerator. It showed the whole family sitting on the couch on the front porch, with Mr. and Mrs. Thompson at the ends, John in the middle, and Rachel lying across their laps. All of them were smiling. They're a bit off-center because when I took the picture, I made Rachel's face the focal point.

I grabbed the picture and ran out the front door. In the garage and facing the bicycles, I realized I'd never be able to reach the pedals on John's. He was more than a head taller than me, most of it leg. So I took Rachel's. The pedals were still a stretch, but I could reach them while on the seat. It also had a lowered center bar, so I had less trouble getting my leg over the top. I could make it work without using the curb or a step. I only had to overlook the fact that it was electric pink. It had a horn to make up for it, though.

For me, logic was as reliable as my unpredictable feelings, meaning not at all. I was receiving nothing. My feelings had fled the scene. Yet my knowledge of Rachel suggested that, logically, she would make her way east five blocks to Penn Avenue, then south to the Coffee Nook at the corner of Penn and Lowry Avenues. It was an easy walk, plus it was a major MTC bus route. Lots of people Rachel went to school with drove Penn Avenue every day.

I rode slowly, tried to observe everything around me, and hoped something would trigger a feeling so I could quit relying on logic.

Logic suggested I turn right at Penn. After having gone south for two blocks, I considered circling every block or cutting down the alleys. I knew Rachel wouldn't use the alleys, though.

At the bus shelter on the southwest corner of Penn and Dowling Avenues, I leaned the bike against the bus stop sign and sat on one of the rock-hard plastic benches. I pivoted on the bench to greet, then avoid the half-inch, fuzzy black spider beside me. I scanned the houses, the streets, Rocket's Car Repair, and More Cushion Upholstery.

The house on the northwest corner of Queen and Dowling Avenues, facing Penn and the bus shelter, had a real estate sign in the front yard and looked as if no one lived there. It was a story-and-a-half Tudor with brick and vinyl siding. The overgrown arborvitae tried to block the windows, and the new owners would probably remove it.

At least, that was Mom's theory on overgrown arborvitae. Get rid of the ugly things and let some light in.

Other than the character that comes from being an older house, the place had no personality. It was neat but nondescript, no fancy decorations or little yard signs. On the other hand, if someone was selling it, why spend a lot of time and money on flowers and personal touches? It wasn't any more interesting than the surrounding houses. I stared for a while, not sure why.

Across the street from it, with the backyard to me, stood a house with old Masonite siding scalloped to look like waves on the sea. The white paint appeared new. A shiny chain-link fence caged a backyard scattered with small children's toys, and a black lab napped on the back steps.

Another small, neat home shared the alley with the house with the kids and the black lab. Through the window, I saw an older couple sitting in the kitchen. Each had a section of newspaper they reached around to lift coffee cups from the table to their lips. Neither looked my way while I watched them.

Between the building and the privacy fence, I was at the wrong angle to see the houses behind Rocket's Car Repair, which shared the corner with the bus shelter.

Rocket's was in an old building. According to Mom, it had been there for years under lots of different names and owners but otherwise hadn't changed much. The two garage doors stood open. In one bay, a car perched on a hoist with an oil drip bucket beneath. The other bay had a car backed in, still on the floor with the hood open. No one appeared to be working on either car.

More Cushion Upholstery was across Penn from Rocket's, facing me and the bus shelter. The lighted sign in the small window next to the door said it was open, but no lights glowed in any of the windows. The building stood back from the sidewalk about two feet. Brown stucco walls displayed patches of horizontal Masonite siding used to reduce the windows from storefront to conventional bedroom-sized. Poured concrete filled the space from the building to the sidewalk, and a few weeds grew in the cracks. A small tree stood flush to the foundation in front of the building. A larger tree grew between the wall and the side pathway. The building blocked my view of any of the houses behind it.

The northeast corner of Penn and Dowling was the main entrance to the Lake Union Cemetery. A tall wrought-iron fence surrounded the rest of it.

I received no feelings from anything I saw.

Disappointed, I remounted the bike and rode to Rocket's open garage doors. I leaned the bike against a metal machine with a tire clamped on top between the two garage doors and walked inside. "Hello?" I called.

"Help ya?" came a voice from inside the office, followed by an African-American man of about sixty-five. He wore coveralls with an oily front as if he'd wiped his hands on his belly, which wasn't all that large but still prominent. Above the pocket, a patch told me his name was Rocket. He walked stiffly, his legs barely bending at the knees. A ball cap had been jammed over part of his three- or four-inch Afro. A beard that grew thicker on one side than the other and had a touch of gray near his chin covered his face.

When he smiled at me, the thicker-beard side of his mouth curved up higher than the other half.

"I'm hoping you can. I'm wondering if you've seen this girl." I held out the family picture and pointed below Rachel's chin.

"Yep, I have," Rocket confirmed. "Is there a problem?"

"She might be missing. I'm trying to find her."

"Nice young woman. Wonderful smile. Pretty, too. Stopped in one day so I could put air in her bike tires." He pointed at Rachel's bike, leaning against his machine. "That looks like the bike."

"I'm sure it is," I admitted. "I borrowed it a few minutes ago."

"Sometimes I see her when she goes by," Rocket mused. "If she sees me, she always waves and smiles. Makes an old man's day when a pretty girl is nice enough to smile at him."

"She's always been nice to me, too," I remarked. "Which is surprising since I'm really a friend of her little brother. I guess she's become my friend, too."

He laughed. "What's your name?"

"Jacob Daniels, but everyone calls me Daniels."

Mom had called me by my last name since Dad died. Prior to that, he had been Daniels, Mom was Sweetie, and I was Jacob. By default, I succeeded him as the dominant household male and became Daniels. I don't know what would have happened if she had found another love and brought another male into the house. However, after that, she only used my first name when I had angered her. Somehow, the rest of the world automatically had no trouble referring to me as Daniels. Or worse things, I'm sure.

"What's her name?" Rocket asked.

"Rachel Thompson."

"Well, Daniels, how long has our friend Rachel been missing?"

"I guess, officially, she isn't. I had a feeling something was wrong, and her mom had a different feeling something was wrong and specifically that it was with Rachel. So, I decided I needed to look for her."

"Can't deny feelings," Rocket declared. "Too powerful."

"I use them a lot. I try never to deny them."

"I use feelings, too. So did my mama," he stated. "She also said you have to be careful how you read them, or you could be wrong and get into a heap of trouble."

"I think I've been lucky so far."

"Mama said there ain't no such thing as luck." He laughed. "I'm not sure I agree with her on that one." He leaned close. "Rachel hasn't gone by here today that I've seen, so as nice as it's been talking with you, you better go back to looking. Don't want nothing bad to happen."

"You're right. I better get moving," I noted. "Thank you, sir, for talking with me. You have a good day."

"If I see Rachel, I'll tell her Daniels and her family are looking for her," Rocket promised. "Good luck to you, Daniels. God's speed."

I decided I needed to cover more ground than I had so far and peddled hard to the Coffee Nook. I leaned the bike against the building and went in. There were no customers, but two people stood behind the counter, leaning and talking. They both met me beneath the "Order

Here" sign. The guy was tall, a little heavy, and a lot soft. He had short brown hair and clear skin. The girl was taller than me, which isn't saying much, and chunky. A purple streak adorned her dark hair under a hair net and a pimple nestled on the side of her nose.

I held up the picture. "Do you know her?" I asked them.

"I do," the guy affirmed. "I go to school with her. That's Rachel Thompson."

"Yeah, it is. Has she been in here today?"

"No, why?"

"Just wondering," I remarked. "I'm trying to help her parents find her. She hasn't reported in as expected." I held the picture in front of the girl.

"I don't know her," she replied.

"Do you remember ever seeing her?" I asked.

"No, but I mostly make coffee. I don't look too close at all the people," she told me. "Especially the girls."

"Okay, well, thanks." I was almost to the door when I turned back to face them. "Any chance I can use a phone?"

"We're not supposed to let anyone use the phone," the guy claimed. "If you're looking for someone, though, I don't see what it will hurt. Come on back here."

I circled the counter and followed them past all the fancy, hissing machines to the office. The girl pointed at the phone on the desk. "Try not to be too long."

I punched in the Thompsons' number. John answered on the second ring.

"It's Daniels. Any word from Rachel?"

"No. Nothing. And it's making me nuts."

"How's your mom doing?"

"She can't sit still. She's been looking through our

phone books, trying to decide who to call," he explained. "Where are you?"

"I'm at the Coffee Nook. I'm going to start back, but I'll probably take a longer route, see if anything clicks."

"Try to be quick."

"Okay," I promised and hung up. I thanked the workers and asked them if Rachel stopped in, to let her use the phone and check in at home.

I took a long, zigzagged route back to the Thompsons', including a few blocks further north and west than their place and along part of Victory Memorial Drive. Nothing clicked. No feelings crept up, no light bulbs went off. I felt lost. Like I had failed her, failed all the Thompsons.

CHAPTER FOUR

<u>Hanley, March 1997</u>

Hanley carefully stepped to the side of the brush pile. The lost little girl had turned into a victim of a crime, and this area of the park and cemetery was now a crime scene. He shone his light on the ground before placing his foot, then leaned until he could reach Latisha's neck. In his gut, he knew the truth, but he needed to check. No pulse.

He straightened, looked at the sky, and drew a deep breath. He reached for his shoulder microphone and depressed the button. "Dispatch, this is Hanley. I'm in the northeast corner of Lake Union Cemetery. I found Latisha Ford. She's DOD." This was one time he liked acronyms. He didn't want to say dead on discovery.

"Roger that," dispatch stated. "Backup en route."

Keeping his feet planted, Hanley pivoted at the waist, held his digital camera in one hand, and used it to record his surroundings. The only portion of Latisha he allowed in his pictures was her foot. Some things shouldn't be recorded. At least not by him. As he zoomed, panned, and clicked, he tried to see if anybody watched or lurked. If he could see anything or anybody that didn't belong.

After he'd bought this camera, one of the smallest and highest-resolution he could find, he had practiced using it with only his left hand. His other hand rested on his unsnapped holster.

When he had photographed everything within a ten-foot radius of himself, he carefully stepped away from Latisha, hoping to disturb nothing as he went. That was even more critical now that the police knew it was a crime scene.

As he reached the paved road in front of the shed, what looked like the rest of the Fourth Precinct arrived. Within minutes, the quiet corner of the cemetery became a circus as crime scene tape was strung and spotlights deployed. The Crime Scene Unit arrived in their custom van. Six lab techs fanned out and began scouring the cemetery and park, hoping for a piece of evidence that would make the investigation easy and quick.

One investigator pulled the memory card from Hanley's camera and downloaded copies of the pictures into a laptop. He handed the camera back to Hanley, put the memory card into an evidence bag, and walked away. Hanley looked at the camera, then checked his uniform pockets and utility belt for another memory card. He didn't find one, so he made sure the camera was turned off and slipped it into his pocket.

He waited on the paved road with Krause and a handful of others. Somebody brought coffee. He really didn't want any, really didn't like coffee, but he held the cup, trying to drive the cold from his bones. The cold he felt from finding the dead little girl and the chills he had while looking for her.

Detectives McLaren and Whitehead with the Violent Crimes Division led him away from the other cops and the crime scene. "We'll be taking the lead on this one," Whitehead told him.

Hanley nodded. He looked for a place to dump the coffee and get rid of the cup. It no longer provided any heat.

"Did you see anything? Anyone?" McLaren asked.

"No," Hanley admitted. "The lab guys have the memory card from my camera. I tried to record everything I could. You'll be able to backtrack my trail following the quarters and the flashlight."

"The lab is on it," McLaren declared. "One of the lab guys told me you did a nice job documenting your trail."

"How did you end up here?" Whitehead asked.

"I tried to think like a teenager," Hanley explained. "They're immortal, never think about danger. They only want an easy way home from school. I followed what could have been a logical route and ended up in the park. I saw signs of a scuffle and followed the trail."

"Excellent work, Richard," McLaren declared.

"Yeah," Whitehead agreed. "Way to stay with it, see it through."

Hanley shrugged. "I got lucky. Unlike that little girl."

McLaren set a big hand on Hanley's arm. "You did your job. Very well, too. Now, we'll do ours. We'll find whoever did this."

"You try to get some rest," Whitehead encouraged. "Try to put it out of your mind. Don't let it haunt you."

"Not too far out of your mind, though," McLaren cautioned. "We'll probably need to ask some more questions."

"Anything I can do to help, let me know," Hanley replied. He looked toward the brush pile. A police photographer used a large-format camera loaded with film to take pictures that would be impossible to alter. Every time the flash lit up the area, the only thing Hanley could see was the boot and leg belonging to Latisha Ford.

CHAPTER FIVE

<u>Daniels, August 2000</u>

Mrs. Thompson stood on the front porch as I pulled Rachel's bicycle into the driveway. She faced slightly south as if she expected Rachel to return from that direction any moment. "Where have you been?" she asked, her arms folded tight across her chest.

"Out looking," I told her.

"Anything?"

"No." I climbed the steps and stood next to her, facing the same way she did. I didn't know why. Maybe it was like getting on an elevator - everybody faces the door.

She was a bit taller than John, which made her considerably taller than me. Her short hair was someplace between John's light brown and Rachel's blonde. She wore dress pants, low heels, and a pale yellow blouse.

"What are we going to do?" she asked.

"Keep looking until we find her," I insisted. "Or she comes home."

She looked at me and tried to smile. "You're right. She'll turn up, and we'll have worried for nothing."

Except I knew, like she did, that we weren't worrying for nothing.

I held the door for Mrs. Thompson, and we walked into the house. John came out of the kitchen. "I listened to the answering machine again. The message really doesn't tell us anything." His dark hair stood up, his eyes wide, nostrils flared. "I don't know what to do." He pushed his glasses into place with his middle finger, then ran both hands through his hair. Except it was more like he pulled it up instead of smoothed it down. "Could you have been wrong? What did you see?"

"I didn't see anything," Mrs. Thompson noted. "That isn't how it works."

He tried to turn, then stopped, acted as if he would turn the other way, and stopped again. "But..."

"John, calm down," she urged. "You panicking isn't going to help us."

"I think it's the only thing I know how to do right now," John stated.

"Come here." She met him in the middle of the room. They hugged and rocked. After a minute or so, she suggested, "Grab the phone book. Let's start calling people."

Mrs. Thompson sat at the kitchen table, appeared to be thinking, then punched in a number. "This is Helen Thompson. Is Peter available?" That would be Mr. Thompson. "I understand. No. No message. Thank you." She closed her eyes and sighed.

She started going between the family phone book,

which was yellow with orange and red flowers, and the Minneapolis White Pages, calling people she thought might know where Rachel was. John paced from the front window to the back door and back. Every few laps, he would step out onto the front sidewalk and look up and down the street as if someone needed to be on sentry duty.

I curled up on the couch and tried to meditate but watched John instead.

The afternoon passed quickly, yet it felt like it lasted forever. Mrs. Thompson was between calls when the phone rang at the same time Mr. Thompson walked in the front door. According to the VCR clock, it was 5:15. Mrs. Thompson managed a smile for her husband as she answered the call. After her greeting, she told the caller, "Rachel's not here now. I'm hoping she's at work." Her brow furled, and her eyes seemed to cloud. "You mean she didn't arrive?" "You're right. That's not like her." "Yes, of course. I'll have her call you as soon as I hear from her. You do the same if you see her first."

She hung up and looked at John and me. "She didn't show up at work." Her voice trembled, and she turned to her husband. "I received a flash. Something has happened to Rachel. We haven't been able to find her. I'm really worried now."

"Where have you looked?" Mr. Thompson asked.

"Daniels looked between here and the Coffee Nook," she explained. "I've called some people. No one has seen her. And that was the theater. She didn't show up for her shift."

"John and I will drive around, past the coffee shops and school, and we'll end up at her work," Mr. Thompson assured her. "Maybe she'll show up by then. You keep calling."

I sat at the kitchen table, watching Mrs. Thompson, my legs pulled up and folded into a lotus. While I didn't close my eyes, I tried to clear my mind, make it open and receptive.

Mrs. Thompson rifled through the phone book until she found a name she wanted and pinned the book to the table with one hand. The other punched in the number as the phone lay on the table. Once she had the number in, she picked up the phone. Sometimes someone answered. They'd talk for a few seconds, then she'd hang up and repeat the process. With every call, she trembled a bit more until she was punching numbers incorrectly and had to start over. She actually completed a few wrong numbers. When she read them back, she was usually off by only one button.

She set the phone on the table directly in front of me. "Answer it if it rings," she told me and left the kitchen. I heard the bathroom door close.

I picked up the phone and called home. "Can you come to the Thompsons'?" I asked.

"Sure," Mom agreed. "Is anything wrong?"

"We can't find Rachel. I think the Thompsons may need you."

"I'm on my way. Should I bring anything?"

Lots of people probably had cell phones, but Mom was one of the few I knew who carried one. The Thompsons had never used one in my presence. I saw people who had pagers and, after they looked at their little screens, went in search of a phone. Mom decided she should have a cell phone for her work as a property manager, and she forwarded our home phone to it when she went out. I suggested she bring it and maybe her charger.

"What about supper?" she asked. "Have the Thompsons eaten anything?"

"I don't think food has even crossed their minds."

"There's no need for anybody to be cooking until we know Rachel is okay," Mom pronounced. "I'll find something on the way."

I set the phone on the table. Mrs. Thompson came into the kitchen and looked at it with red eyes. "I called my mom," I announced. "She's going to come over."

Mrs. Thompson nodded. "I better start some coffee. I know your mom likes it strong, but that doesn't mean she can't have a fresh pot." She opened the refrigerator and stared inside.

"Mom's going to bring something for dinner, too."

"She's so thoughtful. What would we do without her?" Mrs. Thompson fired up the coffee maker, occasionally looking at the phone as if watching it would make it ring. The front of their house faced east, and large trees filled the yard. Shadows in the house began to grow as the trees blocked the setting sun. Mrs. Thompson moved through the house and turned on all of the lights. Then she moved around again, taking quick peeks out the windows.

Someone knocked at the front door, and I ran to answer it. Mrs. Thompson was close behind. I let my mom in the house. She handed me a grocery bag and a jumbo-sized box of roasted chicken. Then she pushed me aside and wrapped her arms around Mrs. Thompson.

"I'm here to help," Mom declared.

"I'm so scared." Mrs. Thompson laid her head on top of Mom's, tears forming at the corners of her eyes.

"I'm sure you are, and that's okay," Mom soothed. "We'll find Rachel."

As they sat at the kitchen table, Mrs. Thompson looked through her phone book, picked a number, and Mom would call it on her cell phone. They didn't hear anything positive back and always asked whoever they spoke with to call if they heard from Rachel or learned where she might be. They left the Thompsons' number so the calls would come back on an open line. Yet the Thompsons' phone sat quietly in the middle of the table.

I wandered off, wondering how I could help. I wished I really was psychic, able to control my abilities so I could receive a message, know Rachel was okay, and take her parents to her. I crept up the stairs, touching everything I thought Rachel might have touched in the years she lived in the house. The light switch, the railing, the school pictures hanging parallel to the stairs. Ascending the stairs was like watching John and Rachel grow up. John on my left, Rachel on my right. John was always the nerd. Rachel started out beautiful and only got better. I straightened a few of her pictures, an excuse to touch them. John's stayed crooked.

I dragged my fingers along the walls as I walked the upstairs hall, hoping someone had left fingerprints I could connect with. I tried to keep my mind open. I even closed my eyes for part of the hallway.

I passed the doors to John's and Rachel's rooms and looked in Mr. and Mrs. Thompson's bedroom in the northwest corner of the second floor. A large window looked out through the upstairs screened-in porch into the backyard and toward Victory Memorial Drive, a block to the west. A door to the porch stood in the corner behind a chair with a quilt draped over it. You would have to move the chair to open the door and go onto the porch, which was actually above the kitchen.

An old, stained-glass window hung from the frame of the large window above a curtain that covered the bottom half. The sun filtered through the trees, across the porch, and into the bedroom through the stained glass. Glimmers of colored light splashed the room and the queen-sized bed. Other than the stained glass, the room contained white and neutral colors, as if to avoid competing with the colored sunlight. Everything appeared neat and dust-free.

Rachel's room occupied the southwest corner. She had a large window and a view but no door to the porch. For the second time in my life, I entered Rachel's bedroom. The first being when I searched the house for her earlier that day. The wall to the porch and the wall opposite were painted white and textured, as Rachel had applied some-thing that dried shiny and reflected light with a feather duster or a broom. The other two walls, a pale blue, reminded me of Rachel's favorite eye shadow.

Her queen-sized bed took up half the room. A dresser and a desk filled most of the other half. Her computer tower sat beside the desk, and the bulky monitor occupied most of the top. A picture of a German Shepard puppy adorned the mouse pad. She had two small, pink books tucked under the edge of the monitor. One was a phone book. The other had a small lock, and I guessed it was a journal or diary. I thought about trying to pick the lock but hadn't touched anything so far. For some reason, that seemed like a better idea.

"Daniels," Mrs. Thompson called. "Are you upstairs?"

I stepped back into the hallway. "Yes, ma'am."

"Would you go into Rachel's room and see if you can find her phone book?" she asked. "I think it's pink."

I returned to Rachel's desk and slid the phone book out without touching the diary. While I wasn't a real psychic, I couldn't decide if leaving fingerprints or learning something about Rachel I shouldn't know was worth the risk. Or which would be worse…learning something or having to explain my fingerprints.

Either way, I knew she wouldn't be happy to come home and find I'd been prowling around her room, touching her stuff. Knowing that did not require any psychic abilities.

I hurried from the room and down the stairs. I handed the phone book to Mrs. Thompson as Mom completed another call. She looked at Mrs. Thompson, who already had the book open, then at me and slightly shook her head.

I wondered when we were supposed to involve the police but was afraid to bring it up. I didn't want to find out how Mrs. Thompson would handle it.

As Mrs. Thompson called out a number and Mom punched buttons, I left the house to sit on the front porch. It was open without any screens and painted to match the outside of the house. I wasn't sure how much it was actually used. Probably only by John, Rachel, and their friends. I guessed the adults would sneak out of their bedroom and use the upstairs screen porch after the kids were in bed.

I went to the wicker couch, folded myself on top of the

cushions, tried to see my breath, and waited. Neither calming nor opening my mind worked. I managed to sit still, an accomplishment in itself, but my mind ran as if it were filmed in slow motion and played back super-fast. The images of all I'd seen during my searches and all I'd experienced as Rachel's friend ran through my brain so fast they made the *Home Alone* kid look calm.

I sat in the dark, ignoring the mosquitoes and the sounds of the neighborhood, when John and Mr. Thompson returned from their search. They didn't see me as they went in the front door. I followed and stopped behind John in time to hear his dad say, "I think it's time to call the police."

Mr. Thompson grabbed the phone off the table and started punching numbers. After a few seconds, he stated, "I'd like to report a missing person." He followed with his name and address. Mom and Mrs. Thompson picked another number from Rachel's phone book, and Mom entered the number into her cell phone. They seemed to be about halfway through the book.

I returned to the porch, smoothed the cushions on the wicker couch, and climbed back into it. John followed a few minutes later and stood against the railing, looking out into the neighborhood.

"Where do you think she could be?" he asked.

"I don't know."

"This isn't good, is it?"

I frowned. "No. It feels bad."

"Can't you find her?"

"I don't have a clue where to start," I confessed. "Or an image or a feeling. Nothing telling me where I should go."

"This is why you were so weird earlier, isn't it?" he asked. "Why I beat you so bad?"

"I think so."

"What are we going to do?" His voice rose in pitch. I couldn't tell in the shadows, but he may have been crying. I understood.

"Until something changes, we're going to let the police do their thing," I told him.

"If that doesn't work?"

"Then we'll do something different. We'll find her." I tried to sound confident. It sure wasn't how I felt.

Rachel was in trouble. That I knew. I had to find her before it was too late. My feelings told me I still had time, but it wouldn't last, so I had to hurry. Or my search for her would quickly become a mission of revenge, and I would want to hurt someone. If they hurt Rachel, they deserved to die. I knew I could do it.

Another thing I should not be thinking right before eighth grade.

CHAPTER SIX

<u>Latisha, March 1997</u>

It creeped out Latisha to see all these people moving around, taking pictures, acting like she was the center of attention but not really seeing her. Had they done this kind of thing so many times that they no longer saw the dead girl?

She knew the cop who found her cared and would see her if she were alive. He had left with a couple of other cops a little while ago. He looked older than when she had first seen him.

A woman in a dark lab coat had one end of a tape measure. She held it against the bottom of Latisha's boot. A man in a lab coat stood at the other end of the tape, moving from tree to tree to the road and to the shed. As he called out measurements, a cop in uniform wrote them on a yellow legal pad.

A Ford Taurus rumbled down the paved road through the cemetery. It had barely stopped before her momma jumped out from behind the steering wheel. She ran past the police cars filling the cemetery. As she approached the police tape, she looked like a sprinter about to cross the finish line. Three cops caught her while letting out a chorus of "You can't..." and "Please don't..." and "Stop, ma'am..."

Latisha wanted to shove them away and let her momma through.

"Is that my... Let me in there," Latisha's mother demanded. "I've got to see her."

A tall, thin black man with a neatly trimmed mustache and a touch of gray at the temples stepped up beside Latisha's mother. "I'm Inspector Johnson. And who might you be?" Latisha liked his smooth, musical voice.

"I'm Rose Ford."

"Ms. Ford, there is no easy way to say this, but I believe we found your daughter. I'm sorry to say she is dead."

"Are you sure?"

"Yes, ma'am. Reasonably certain," Johnson replied. "I'm sorry."

Rose Ford's knees folded. Inspector Johnson caught her easily and lifted her to her feet. Latisha watched tears run down her momma's cheeks. "I want to see my baby. When can I see my baby?" Rose asked.

"We'll let you see her when she's ready. You want to wait a bit, but we're looking out for her until then."

CHAPTER SEVEN

<u>Daniels, August 2000</u>

A Minneapolis Police squad car pulled up in front of the house without any flashing lights. It parked against the curb, and the engine shut off. A uniformed officer got out, looked up and down the street, around the neighborhood, and walked up the sidewalk.

John got to his feet. "Hello."

"Hi. I'm Officer Krause. Somebody here called the police."

"That would be my dad," John confirmed. "He's in the house. C'mon in."

John opened the door, stepped through, then held it open. Officer Krause followed John into the house. He glanced at me as he crossed the threshold.

I rose from the wicker couch and started for the door. I entered and walked into the living room as Mr. Thompson announced, "Our daughter is missing."

"Maybe she's off on a lark or something," Krause

suggested. "Found something to distract her, made her forget to call."

"Rachel is not the type," Mrs. Thompson insisted.

"Sometimes kids get a wild idea. It takes root and makes them do things out of the ordinary," Krause claimed.

As he talked, Krause kept his thumbs hooked in his belt, the right one barely an inch from his gun. It looked casual, but I suspected he was ready for anything. He had thinning, sandy blond hair a few inches long, parted on the side and pushed back so it stayed off his face. The back was a little longer and curled at his collar. He was easily the biggest person in the room, a few inches taller than Mr. Thompson and quite a bit heavier. He looked as if he had softened through the years. Not the condition I expected for a cop.

"Let's start at the beginning. Why do you think she is missing?" He pulled a small notebook from his back pocket.

Mr. and Mrs. Thompson told the story of the day's events and the trip to Rachel's work. In the middle, they included who Mom and I were and why we were there. Mr. Thompson played the answering machine recording, and Mom and Mrs. Thompson listed the people they had called.

"You've certainly been proactive," Krause commented. "Nobody has seen her since this morning?"

"No," Mr. Thompson confirmed. "No one."

"Can I see her room?" Krause asked.

"Of course." Mr. Thompson led Krause upstairs.

From the bottom of the stairs, I heard Krause ask, "Has anyone been in here?"

"I don't believe so," Mr. Thompson stated.

"I have," I called.

They came to the top of the stairs, and I continued. "I brought down Rachel's phone book. I tried not to touch anything."

"I was for a few minutes, too," Mrs. Thompson reported.

Krause nodded and went back to Rachel's room. A few minutes later, they came back downstairs. Mr. Thompson stood next to his wife. He was a few inches taller, his hair similar to John's. He still wore the navy suit he'd worn to work that morning. Mrs. Thompson laid a hand on his arm and leaned into him.

Krause addressed me. "They said you were looking, too. Where did you look?"

I nodded. "I rode Rachel's bike to the Coffee Nook and stopped at Rocket's Car Repair. On the way back, I took a bunch of side streets, hoping I'd stumble into her. Finally, I covered part of the parkway. I've shown this to Rocket and the kids at the Coffee Nook." I handed him the picture I had taken off the refrigerator. "None of them saw her today."

"Does she have a boyfriend?" Krause asked.

"No," Mrs. Thompson declared.

"Yeah," John countered. "His name is Eric."

"She never told me she had a new boyfriend." Mrs. Thompson's head shook, and her face reddened.

"She's been hiding this one," John told her. "You didn't like the last one."

"He was too old," Mr. Thompson noted. His lip turned

down, and the muscles in his jaw worked. If I had been closer, I might have heard his teeth grind.

"This one is younger, closer to her age, but she didn't want to take the chance. That's really all I know. She was afraid if I knew more, I'd blackmail her."

"Does anybody know more about Eric?" Krause asked.

"Eric Bennett will be the starting quarterback on this year's football team," I piped in. "The one Mrs. Thompson didn't like was the starting quarterback from two years ago. I don't know his name. He's attending St. Thomas now. They weren't together very long, though."

"Why not?" Krause asked.

"I don't know. I only know he told her it wasn't working, and he dumped her."

"When was that?" Mrs. Thompson asked.

"It's been a while," I noted. "She was down for a few days, didn't say much. Then she must have found Eric because she was back to being herself."

"Must've been a couple of months ago, closer to when school let out," John remarked. "I thought she was...you know..." He flushed crimson. "Or she was being normal, then she got nice again. That always makes me nervous. Like she's up to something."

"You can let people be nice to you," I told him. "It's okay if someone likes you. Even if it is your family."

"Can we focus here?" Krause asked.

"We are," I stated. "This is kind of how we figure things out."

John nodded, and Krause sighed.

I continued. "Eric drives a red Ford Mustang. When he's not with Rachel, he's usually at the Accelerometer

Fitness Club on Forty-Second and Lyndale, surrounded by the team."

"Have you talked with anybody named Eric Bennett?" Krause asked Mom and Mrs. Thompson.

Mrs. Thompson shook her head.

"I don't remember seeing that name in the phone book," Mom revealed. "So, no, we didn't call any Eric Bennett."

"Okay," Krause remarked. "We'll track him down."

"You may also want to find Riley Cummings and Brandon Humphries," I suggested.

"Who are they?" Krause asked.

"Brandon is another former boyfriend. Riley is his friend."

"Why do you think I should talk to them?" Krause asked.

"I think Riley pushed Rachel down the stairs at the mall last year," I reported.

"What?" Mr. Thompson's hands came up to about waist-high, clenched into fists.

"Back when she broke her leg, when she fell down the stairs at Ridgedale. I believe she was pushed," I elaborated.

"Why would this Riley push her down the stairs?" Krause asked.

"Because Brandon told him to. He was still mad at her from when they broke up. I think Brandon intended to weasel back into her life by showing he could take care of her."

"Was this ever reported?" Krause asked.

"No."

"Why not?" Krause asked.

47

"This is the first we've heard of it," Mr. Thompson announced. "Why didn't somebody tell us?"

"Because there was no way to prove it," I told him.

"Why are you telling us now?" Krause asked.

"Because when you ask about Rachel and tell them I gave you their names, they're going to tell you I assaulted them."

"Did you?" Mom asked.

"Brandon twice, Riley once," I admitted.

John shook his head. "Ah, Daniels. What the hell are you doing?"

"It's going to come out," I stated. "I might as well start the conversation. I have nothing to hide."

"So tell me about it," Krause invited.

"The first time, Brandon was forcing himself on Rachel. It was in the living room, on the couch. I was headed for the bathroom, and I heard her tell him no."

The room went quiet. Mrs. Thompson sagged into a chair and sniffled. Mom gave me the stare. Mr. Thompson rocked from side to side. It didn't look as if his eyes were focused on anything.

"I suggested Brandon listen to her, and he hit me. Then he hit Rachel. So I wrecked his knee," I offered.

Krause had stopped taking notes to stare at me.

"The second time, I ran into Brandon and Riley when they were crossing the Loring Elementary playground," I went on. "I confronted them about Rachel's fall and convinced them nothing better happen to her ever again."

"How did you do that?" Krause asked.

"They were kind of a mess when I last saw them," I noted.

48

"But now something has happened to Rachel," John declared.

"We don't know that," Krause advised.

"Which is why you better talk to them," I suggested. "Soon."

Krause thanked us for our help and all the information. He said he'd get the word out, but the police usually didn't pursue a missing person too seriously for the first day unless there was evidence suggesting abduction. However, if nobody heard from her soon, he was sure the entire force would be looking, and a couple of detectives would probably be by to ask more questions.

What John and I had known all day wasn't evidence. Now we had to wait.

CHAPTER EIGHT

Mom and I rode home in silence. She swung down the alley and into the garage, where she shut off the engine but did not open the car door. I waited for her to make the first move.

"I didn't like what I heard tonight," she remarked.

"I knew you wouldn't. But it had to be done."

"Not that way, it didn't," she insisted. "There are other ways to protect the people we care about."

"Without proof, it would have been my word against the two of them," I told her. "Even Rachel wasn't sure. I asked her."

"Still…"

"You've always told me we need to look out for others. Great Grandma Nan told me I need to help people."

"Is she still coming around?"

"Yep. Too often, if you ask me."

"There are still other ways to help people."

"I know, and violence should always be the last choice. You and Mr. Lee have taught me well," I assured her. "Some people aren't able to learn unless you make it perfectly clear, though." I waited for Mom to say something. She didn't. "I'm only trying to help people. Sometimes I have to do it by helping others understand that some of the things they do won't be allowed."

"If you're going to be this way, I have two requests," Mom claimed.

"Okay," I agreed. "Tell me, and I'll try."

"Tell me when you get into an altercation, so I'm not surprised when I hear it from the police."

"I'll do what I can. What's the other?"

"Be careful."

"Always."

CHAPTER NINE

The next morning, Mom and I returned to the Thompsons' house. Mom and Mrs. Thompson went through the phone books again, calling everyone they had already talked to the day before. I'm not sure if Mr. Thompson had slept. His brown hair stood straight up, his eyes were red, his face unshaven. He wore a Minnesota Twins tee shirt and jeans. He had moved a chair so he had a perfect view of both the front and back doors. His head turned from one side to the other, his chin resting in his hand, which seemed to turn when his head did so his fingers always pointed at the door he looked at.

At some point, John had gone to their basement and dug through the games. He sat on the porch, fingers resting on a plastic platen, willing the Ouija board to give him a message.

I took my place on the wicker couch and meditated, hoping to receive something. It went poorly. I watched John and listened to him mumble questions to the spirits avoiding the game. All of a sudden, he yelled, "Where's my sister, you bastard?" and threw the board off the porch into the middle of the front yard.

"I hope you didn't lose the needle," I commented.

"Who gives a fuck?" John spat. "I'm surrounded by psychics, believe in ESP with all my heart, every corner of my brain knows it exists, and a fucking Ouija board won't even talk to me. What's the point?" He jumped to his feet and ran into the house.

I followed him. He'd gone into the kitchen, where Mom and Mrs. Thompson still worked the phone. Mrs. Thompson wrapped him in her arms and pulled him into her lap. He didn't fit very well, but neither seemed to care.

Mom got to her feet, whispered something to Mrs. Thompson, and crossed the kitchen to where I stood. "Let's run to the store," she suggested.

I followed her out and, after picking up the Ouija board with the needle somehow still in the center of the platen, climbed in the car.

"I thought they needed a few minutes," Mom remarked. "It gives us a chance to get some food, make sure they keep eating." We went to our favorite Chinese restaurant, which happened to be in one of the buildings Mom owned.

My father died when I was four. His job was in marketing for General Mills, and quite often, he worked late. Dad was driving through Golden Valley when he saw a house on fire. He went in and pulled out three people. They told him there was still one inside, and Dad went back in as the fire trucks arrived. He was on his way back out, carrying a little boy when the floor collapsed beneath them.

Mom and Dad had already invested in a few properties

in the Camden neighborhood of North Minneapolis, plus a couple in New Hope and Robbinsdale. Mom used the money from the insurance Dad's job provided and a few policies he had picked up to buy more properties. Some were houses, but quite a few were strip malls, like the one that housed the Flying Dragon, and multiple-unit commercial buildings. Like the one that was home to Mr. Lee's martial arts school where I was a student.

The Flying Dragon had barely opened, and there weren't any other customers. We went in, and Mom ordered a few dishes. I sat at a table and drank a Coke while Mr. Yang did the cooking, and Mom talked to Mrs. Yang. Mom told me one time that it didn't make sense to support other businesses when her rent income depended on the success of the businesses renting from her. Every time we patronized them, it gave her another chance to stop in, see how things were going, and look over her building.

We were most of the way back to the Thompsons when Mom mentioned, "You've been awful quiet."

"I don't know what to do," I stated. "I want to help, but how?"

"I don't know either," Mom admitted. "I think we're doing what we can by being with them, letting them know we care."

"That isn't helping Rachel, though."

"I know, but we can only do what we can do. You're not in control."

"Yeah, I know," I declared. "And I hate it."

"You sound like your father."

CHAPTER TEN

Hanley, March 1997

Richard Hanley stood in the back corner of the room, facing Latisha Ford's casket. He wore a dark suit, a white shirt, and a dark tie. A small woman approached him.

"Hello," she greeted.

"Hello, ma'am."

"Do I know you?" Her voice was soft, low with a touch of gravel.

"I don't believe so," he told her. "I'm Richard Hanley."

"I'm Rose Ford." One of her hands held a balled-up tissue, the other a rosary. "Did you know my daughter?"

"Not really," Hanley admitted. "I'm a cop. I wanted to pay my respects."

"You're the one who found my little girl," she noted.

He was surprised. Hanley didn't think anybody outside the force knew. "Yes, ma'am," he replied. "I only wish I'd have found her sooner."

"What's done is done. It's God's will. I don't believe

she'd have been alive if you had found her any sooner than you did."

"That's probably true. Doesn't mean I can't wish it was different."

"No, it don't," she agreed. "Thank you, Richard. Thank you for caring."

Hanley shuffled his feet and clasped his hands behind him.

"You're going to find the monster that took my baby, aren't you, Richard?"

"We're doing everything we can, ma'am."

"No. I mean you."

"I'd love to say yes to that," Hanley claimed. "Unfortunately, I haven't been on the force long enough. The detectives are working the investigation now. I'm doing my usual job, but I'm available if they need me."

"You'll find him, and you'll stop him," Rose insisted. She turned and walked toward the casket. "I know you will."

CHAPTER ELEVEN

Daniels, August 2000

A couple of cars sat in front of the Thompsons' when we returned. One was obviously a police car. The other probably was, too. Mom and I each carried a bag of food into the house and found everybody sitting in the living room. Mr. Thompson was in the same chair as when we left. John and Mrs. Thompson huddled on the couch, holding hands. Officer Krause stood to the side, not too far into the room.

A thin man in a charcoal gray suit with a wide red nose and thinning, close-cropped brown hair sat beside Mr. Thompson. Another man in a navy suit with a bit of a paunch, a double chin, and gray buzz-cut hair occupied a chair pulled up next to the couch. They both stood when we walked in.

"Hello, Mrs. Daniels," Krause greeted. He looked at me. "How you doing, kid?"

"Hello, Officer Krause," Mom replied. "I wish I could say it was good to see you again."

He nodded and looked at his shoes.

The man standing beside Mr. Thompson pulled out his wallet and flipped it open to show us a badge. "I'm Detective McLaren. He's my partner, Detective Whitehead."

"I'm Bethany Daniels. This is my son, Jacob," Mom replied. "Should we come back later?"

"No, ma'am," Whitehead stated. "We're just following up. Officer Krause gave us the details of your conversation yesterday. We're here to say this is an official missing persons case, and we have all of our resources working on it."

"I'm glad," Mom offered. "As I'm sure the Thompsons and Officer Krause told you, we were convinced that Rachel was missing yesterday."

Mr. Thompson continued to look from the front door to the back as he had earlier. He didn't seem to be listening.

"Rest assured, Officer Krause worked late into the night with the information you provided," McLaren reported. "He's done a good job and got a lot of the preliminary legwork out of the way."

"That's good to hear," Mom responded. "What is your area of expertise?"

McLaren looked at the Thompsons as if hoping they weren't listening. "We're with Violent Crimes, ma'am."

"Really?" Mom asked. "Has there been anything to indicate there's been a violent crime committed?"

"No, ma'am," McLaren admitted. "But with missing persons, time is of the essence. It's all hands on deck."

Mom nodded. "I think I can speak for the Thompsons and say we're relieved that Officer Krause continued to pursue it. Dare I ask why you weren't here already this morning? Following up, checking on things?"

"I was out, continuing from last night, working with the information we had, ma'am," Krause stated. "I wasn't alone, either. We had a lot of officers on the street looking. Some of them came in on their day off to help."

John had sagged, so his head rested on his mother's shoulder. They both stared at their hands.

"Thank you and all those who were helping." Mom started for the kitchen. "However, I'm sure you can understand our frustration."

"Yes, ma'am," they replied, almost in unison.

"We were about to have some lunch," Mom announced. "It's from the Flying Dragon. I know there's more than enough. Would you like a bit before you head out to resume the search?"

"Thank you, Mrs. Daniels," McLaren declared. "But no, we need to meet up with some of the others, keep this going."

"How about a chicken wing?" Mom asked. "You might be able to eat it while you work."

Krause raised a hand. "If it's from the Flying Dragon, I don't mind if I do. I love their food. It's always excellent. And I can drive while eating a wing." He ventured into the kitchen, and I followed with the other bag of food.

Mom opened a box, pulled out a wing, wrapped it in a paper towel, and handed it to Krause. She extracted a few more and wrapped them as well. "Detectives, please. I insist."

They both smiled. "If you insist." Whitehead took a wing.

"We'll check back with you later." McLaren also grabbed one and led the other two toward the door.

"We're counting on you," Mom reminded them. They turned and looked back, but she was busy setting the table.

Once she had all the containers open, she went to the living room and took Mr. Thompson's hand. "You need to keep your strength up. Come eat." She led him to the table and sat him in a chair. I'm not sure he was really there. She took the reluctant Mrs. Thompson and John by the hands and had to pull them from the couch so she could get them into kitchen chairs as well.

When none of them reached for anything, Mom started dishing. She talked the whole time, telling them about the Yang family and the Flying Dragon, what each of the dishes was, and why she liked them. If the Thompsons hadn't started eating, she probably would have put forks in their hands and made them. All three moved mechanically. They may not have tasted anything.

Krause was right, though. The Flying Dragon's food was always excellent, and this time it might have been better than normal.

CHAPTER TWELVE

After not much lunch, Mr. Thompson returned to his chair. John snuck up to Rachel's room, curled into a fetal position on her bed, and fell asleep. Mom and Mrs. Thompson worked the phones again. They apologized for bothering people more than once but told whoever answered that they couldn't give up.

I tried some meditation, did some yoga, and picked up some sticks lying in the yard and a little garbage from the street. I couldn't sit any longer. When Mom went to use the bathroom, I met her in the hall. "I'm taking Rachel's bike to go look for her. "I don't know what else to do, but I can't do nothing."

"Okay," Mom allowed. "Don't be gone too long, and be careful."

"I know. I will."

I rode at a casual pace, wanting to see whatever I might pass. I circled the block. Then a few blocks. I went to the main intersections to sit and watch. At a faster pace, I rode past Rocket's Car Repair. Faster yet, I biked past the Coffee

Nook, then circled back to the house and went in the other direction to fly past the Accelerometer Fitness Club. I received no signs, messages, or feelings I needed to follow. Where was this supposed gift when I needed it? I pedaled hard and took its absence as further evidence I was not psychic.

I stopped near the rear of the Lake Union Cemetery. I caught my breath, let my heart rate settle and my sweat dry. Then I leaned over the handlebars and clamped my eyes shut. A few tears squeezed from the corners. I opened my eyes in time to see the tears fall into the dust, leaving little impact craters. After a sigh and a sniffle, I scanned the cemetery, then looked at the clear sky. "I don't know what to do. I don't know where to look," I remarked to whoever was listening. "A little help would be appreciated."

It ended up being a few hours before I returned to the Thompson house as the delivery woman from Fine's World of Fine Pizza was leaving. For this meal, Mr. Thompson stayed in his chair. Mom brought him a plate of slices.

John had remained in Rachel's room the entire time I was gone. I woke him, followed him downstairs, and watched as he took a plate of pizza out to the front porch.

Mrs. Thompson took a slice, stared at it, then picked the top off and ate the meat and cheese. "Rachel loves Fine's pizza. I think she'd like to have a job there so she could eat it anytime." She stared at the crust for a moment, then began to cry.

Mom put an arm around her. They slid into a rocking motion, like what Mom used with me when I woke from one of my frequent nightmares, and she'd try to calm me.

I took a few slices and headed to the front porch.

"They will find her, won't they?" John asked.

"Of course."

"Sometimes they don't, you know," he noted. "Sometimes they never find the body."

"They're not looking for a body," I corrected. "They're looking for Rachel."

"Why don't I have an ability like you and Mom?" John asked.

"I don't know," I admitted. "You're the only one who claims I'm psychic, though."

"I've seen your ability at work. It's real. You're psychic."

"If it's real, how come it isn't working now?" I asked. "Why can't I find Rachel?"

"It's because you don't know how to control it," John insisted. "If you spent more time training your mind the way you do your body, you'd learn. And you'd be able to help regular people all the time."

"I can't find Rachel because I can't control what I don't have. I'm not psychic."

"No, but you are full of shit. Quit denying it, embrace it. Maybe that will help. Tell yourself, 'I am a psychic.' You know, positive reinforcement stuff. If you think it, it will happen."

"And how is that working for you?"

"I don't have a gift like you do, so nothing is going to work on me."

"I think you might be wrong," I told him. "I have a feeling you might be as psychic as I am."

"Fuck you."

"You've been swearing quite a bit the last couple of days," I observed.

"I'm under stress. It's natural, given the circumstances."

"I suppose it is," I conceded. "I wouldn't let it become a habit, though. Rachel won't be happy. She'll think you're uncivilized."

"As long as she comes back, she can think anything she wants about me," John claimed. "Wow. You'd think I like having a sister or something."

"Something. Don't worry. I won't tell her."

"Thanks."

"I won't tell her you were in her room, either."

"Yeah, that would be bad," John admitted. "What did you do?"

"I went searching. I took her bike again, rode around. I got nothing."

"I don't know what to do," he stated.

"I don't either. I guess we just keep believing."

John smirked. "I believe, I believe. I believe I'll have some more pizza before she comes home and eats the rest."

"I believe I'll join you." And thought maybe I'd further explore real prayer. It couldn't hurt.

CHAPTER THIRTEEN

Hanley, May 1998

Richard Hanley parked the squad car in front of the house, then went through the open gate and up the sidewalk. He placed a foot on the wooden bottom step, and it creaked. The man installing a new dead bolt lock turned to face him, eyes narrowed, brows drawn together.

"Is there a problem, Officer?" the man asked.

"You must be Mr. Ford," Hanley stated.

"I am." He straightened to his full six foot six and looked at the cop. "I ask again, is there a problem, Officer?"

"No, sir, not at all. I'm Richard Hanley."

"Ah, Officer Hanley. Call me Samuel." Ford smiled and extended a large hand. "My wife told me about you. Says you're going to find the monster that stole our daughter."

"I'm trying, sir. I'm still looking." Hanley went up a step so he was one below Samuel, then shook his hand. "I didn't meet you before. I'd like to express my condolences, sir."

"Thank you, Officer."

"Please, call me Rich."

"I can do that, Rich, but tell me. What makes you think you're going to find this piece of shit? None of the detectives I talk to display your confidence."

"They've followed every lead that's come in and so far gotten nowhere. We keep looking, though. We're not going to quit."

"I know. But I also know they have fresh murders to worry about. Murders they may be able to solve sooner."

"Yes, sir, it's a bad year to be a Violent Crimes detective. They're not getting any rest."

" I'm not helping any. I'm staying after them, making sure they don't forget," Samuel declared. "You haven't answered my question, though, Rich. Why are you different?"

"Actually, sir, it's your wife. She's convinced I'm going to do it, and I don't want to let her down."

"No, she's not someone you want to disappoint," Samuel concurred. "She'll let you know, too."

Hanley nodded. "I'm sure she will. I didn't mean to interrupt your work. I only wanted to stop by and see if you were all okay."

"As okay as we can be," Samuel professed.

"Samuel, who you talking to?" Rose Ford asked. She stepped to the door and looked out. "Well, hello, Richard. I didn't know you were here."

"I stopped by a couple of minutes ago," Hanley told her. "I've been bothering your husband."

"I knew he found an excuse to stop working. I just didn't know it was you."

"How did you know I wasn't working?" Samuel asked.

"Because there weren't no cussing going on," Rose retorted.

"I've been better," Samuel insisted.

"You been trying." They both laughed. "Oh, we haven't done that in a while," Rose remarked. "It's been hard to see the positive in things."

Hanley nodded and looked at the porch.

Rose reached inside the door and came out with a picture. "I found an extra the other day," she noted. "I thought maybe you should have one."

Hanley looked at the smiling face of Latisha Ford and her Siamese cat from a picture that may have been taken for school. Latisha wore a bright blue top with a matching ribbon in her hair. "Thank you, ma'am. I appreciate it."

"Oh, it's not a kindness," Rose told him. "It's to keep you remembering."

"I'm not having any trouble remembering your daughter. I have plenty of images trapped in my head. This is the first one I have with Latisha smiling, though." He looked up from the picture and smiled at the Fords. "So, in a way, yeah. This is a kindness."

"Well, I'm glad I could help," Rose replied. "Would you like to stay for dinner, Richard?"

"Thank you. I appreciate the offer, and I'd love to, but I'm afraid I can't," Hanley claimed. "I've only got a few minutes for a break, and I used them to stop by and see you. I can't be out of my area too much longer."

"Maybe another time," Samuel invited.

"Yes, please," Rose agreed.

"Thank you. That would be wonderful." Hanley looked at the picture again, then slowly turned and started to move away. "I'll see you soon." He gestured with the picture. "Thanks again."

Rose nodded.

"Is dinner ready?" Samuel asked.

"Not until the lock is finished," Rose answered. "Go back to your cussing."

CHAPTER FOURTEEN

Daniels, August 2000

Rachel hadn't come home, and no one had called. We simply waited. Officer Krause stopped by around ten to ask if we'd heard anything. In spite of lots of volunteers and search parties and people who wanted to think they were contributing, no sign of Rachel had been found.

We stayed until close to midnight.

"All this waiting is exhausting," Mom stated.

"Yeah," I agreed. "Remind me not to do things that make me wait."

"Let's try to sleep in tomorrow," she suggested. "Maybe the Thompsons will get some rest, too."

"It's worth a try." As long as Great Grandma Nan left me alone.

I was excited, as I should have been. I was in bed with Rachel Thompson.

We were both awake, aware of what we were doing. It was voluntary, intentional. We were not sneaking.

Too bad it was only a dream.

In all the dreams Rachel had passed through, we had never talked or touched. We had never been close to each other, much less in a bed.

So I was nervous, too. As I should have been. For one thing, I didn't want to mess up an opportunity like this.

Yet we were in my mom's bed. I recognized the simple headboard, the flowered dust ruffle and comforter, and the stuffed bear sitting behind Rachel. I gave it to Mom as a Mother's Day present when I was five. I used her money to pay for it. The bear was brown with button eyes, a plastic nose, and a heart held between its front paws. It had sat in that spot since. Mom and I tried to respect each other's space and generally only went into the other's room if we were both there. She hadn't cleaned mine in years. She had me change my own sheets, vacuum, and dust for myself, put away my own clothes. But she wasn't here, and I knew she wouldn't understand my having a girl in her bed.

I had visions of Eric Bennett coming over. Besides a strong throwing arm, Rachel's latest had a jealous streak the width of a football field. He also seemed to enjoy hurting people, especially males who went near Rachel. They'd been dating only a short time, too. Imagine how he would react to our being in bed. It would be another confrontation between me and one of her boyfriends. A no-win situation if there ever was one.

Plus, Mom's bed was in Mr. and Mrs. Thompson's bedroom. I didn't know how. Dreams did that sometimes.

The light shined through the stained-glass window beside the upstairs screen porch door and played across Rachel's skin and blonde hair. It cast shadows from the outline of a flower that looked like spider webs by the time they landed on her, separating sections of red from the flower's petals and adding color to her skin. I'd only looked in their room once. Somehow, I didn't think they'd appreciate me being in their room. Especially with their daughter. In a bed.

Still, when Rachel smiled at me, I could almost forget all that. Almost. My nervousness and all those things together nagged at the back of my mind, hinting I should go in a different direction. Yet I was young enough and excited enough, which made me stupid enough to overlook the risks. I wanted to know what would happen next. What I was supposed to do.

Not that I had much choice. I'd learned early in life that sometimes dreams couldn't be changed or avoided, no matter how I tried.

Taking the coward's route, I lay there and enjoyed the view. Her eyes, blue with flecks of gold, sparkled like always. Beneath the incredibly long lashes was her favorite pale blue eye liner with a hint of glitter. Her nose, with freckles I could count on my fingers, leaned a little to the left. I had once wondered if her nose tipping like that would make it easier to look into her eyes as I kissed her. I had never gotten close enough to find out. Pale pink lip gloss covered her moist lips. I couldn't tell if she had on any other makeup, but I never thought she needed it.

She looked closely at my face, skin, and hair. When she examined my eyes, watched me watching her, she looked deep into my soul. Knew every thought I'd ever had about her. My breath caught.

I lay on my left side. She reached out with her left hand. Her painted nails extended beyond the tips of her fingers by about an eighth of an inch, except for the ragged nail on her little finger, like she had broken it and chewed off the rest. I knew she hadn't, though. Every chance she got, Rachel hounded me to quit chewing my nails. She often held hers up so I could see how perfect they were, examine the paint job and the sparkle. She'd offer to paint mine.

The swirls of her fingerprints were easy to see as if they were magnified. A scar marked the side of her first finger, just past the first knuckle. She'd sliced it while cleaning vegetables, a reminder of the time I went with her and her family to the emergency room so she could get stitches.

Rachel's fingers slid along my hair. That, and her closeness, made my skin tingle and turn to gooseflesh. Except her fingers kind of dragged, like something between her skin and my hair messed up the caress. She leaned forward and kissed my cheek. I was surprised at how moist her lips, her kiss, had been. She laughed when I reached up and laid my fingers on the spot she had kissed. Smiled as I moved my hand away and looked at it.

My fingertips had picked up a spot of blood from my cheek. From where Rachel had kissed me. I was sure I had smeared it. I wiped the blood off my fingers onto my mom's comforter.

I reached up and touched her cheek. When I looked at my fingertips again, they were once more covered with blood. My fingers moved down and touched her lips. She pressed a kiss against them. More blood. Her pink tongue snaked out between her lips. It slid down my finger and onto the side of my hand. Her tongue left a smear of blood everywhere it touched.

CHAPTER FIFTEEN

The hall light flicked on, then Mom's shadow stepped through my bedroom doorway. "Daniels, are you okay?" she asked. "You screamed."

"Yeah. I'm fine." I reached toward my feet, snagged the sheet, and pulled it back onto the bed and up to my chin, though sweat soaked both me and the sheet. "It was only a nightmare."

I wished it was. The usual things, I could handle. Storms, monsters, bullies. Even visits from Great Grandma Nan. This one was different, though.

Mom was used to me having nightmares. They'd been a constant my entire life. I don't believe she noticed, but they seemed more frequent and extreme during April, the month Dad died. He was never in them, and I barely remembered him, but somehow, the time of year still affected me.

Rachel, on the other hand, had been in my dreams. But never like this.

"Well, shake it off and go back to sleep," Mom told me.

"Remember, we're sleeping in. Good night, Daniels." She headed back to bed.

I looked at the alarm clock. It was 4:06. In spite of being tired and wanting to sleep, I lay awake and thought about Rachel. While we hoped for the best, had faith, wanted to believe, I knew things were no longer going to work out for the positive. And I hated it.

My breath hung up in my chest, and a few tears squeezed from my eyes.

When I finally crawled out of bed, the sun was up. However, most of the neighborhood still slept. Including Mom. I got dressed, did the usual morning things, and went into the kitchen. I stared into the refrigerator for a few minutes before I realized I didn't want to eat. I rambled around the house a bit longer, then wrote Mom a note telling her I would be at John's.

Mr. Thompson was on the front porch when I arrived, picking up his newspaper. As he turned it, I could see Rachel on the front page. Someone had asked the media for help. Rachel had been the subject of most of the news programs the day before, which brought out the volunteers, and now the newspaper, which only ran in the morning, had joined in. "Good morning," I greeted. In spite of my nightmare and knowing the truth, I managed a smile.

I followed Mr. Thompson into the house. He threw the newspaper on the coffee table, Rachel side up, then took his spot in the chair he'd occupied for the last two days.

My age may have been a factor, and in spite of my personal agony, I could not imagine what Mr. Thompson felt and what was going through his mind. I knew things would never be the same at the Thompson house. Like losing Dad had changed everything for Mom and me.

I went up the stairs, stepped into Rachel's room, and looked around. Nothing had changed since I had last been there.

I crossed into John's room and sat on the edge of his bed. Clothes were piled in the corner, near the dresser, as if they had almost been put away. John usually read a few books at a time. Some of it adult-level science stuff, a lot of it adult-level parapsychology stuff. For fun, he read horror, science fiction, and lots of stories involving extrasensory perception. More parapsychology stuff. Pictures and posters from the *Star Wars* films and his favorite *Star Trek* series, *Deep Space Nine*, decorated the room. I realized for the first time that Carrie Fisher in her Princess Leia bikini and Terry Farrell as Jadzia Dax hung so he could always see one as he lay on either side in bed.

I said John's name three times before he stirred. When he muttered something, I told him, "I dreamed about Rachel."

John was instantly awake. He squinted in my direction as his right hand groped the nightstand, feeling for his glasses. After he found them and jammed them onto his face, he asked, "What did you dream?" His glasses twisted where they crossed his nose. One bow went up into his brown hair, the other into his ear. He didn't seem to notice.

"I don't remember exactly," I declared. He didn't need to know more. The details wouldn't have helped. "I only remember dreaming about Rachel."

"You're so full of shit. What did you dream?"

"No, really." I'd never told him about Rachel appearing

in dreams before. "She kind of passed through, along the edge of one spot. I really don't remember."

"This is a sign. You can find her, Daniels. I know you can." He bounded out of bed and scrambled for his clothes.

"How do you figure?" I asked and shook my head. "What makes you think I can find her when the police can't?"

John gave me the "duh" look, telling me I was missing something simple and obvious. "Because you're psychic. Why do I have to keep reminding you? You find things. It's what you do. It's your gift."

I wanted to say I didn't want to be the psychic. Then I realized his mom probably felt that way too. We are what we are. We do what we have to.

After John had dressed, we started out. His mom was in Rachel's room, straightening her bed. His dad was still manning his post. Neither of them seemed to notice us as we left.

I told myself we were searching for Rachel, but I had no idea where she might be and where we might find her. So I walked, and John followed along. Trust and faith can be dangerous things.

Thanks to the nightmare, I did not feel good about any of this.

We made our way east to Penn Avenue and turned south. At the corner of Penn and Dowling, we stopped at the bus shelter in front of Rocket's Car Repair. I looked around, and John watched me. Nothing interesting was happening in the Lake Union Cemetery or the More Cushion Upholstery shop. Inside Rocket's, I saw a pair of legs leaning into an engine compartment, the top half of the person lost in shadow, as if they weren't entirely there. For a long moment, my gaze remained on the house for sale on the corner of Queen and Dowling. Whatever held my attention the other day had disappeared. It was only an empty house.

John and I continued south on Penn. We stopped at the Coffee Nook and bought bottles of water. John also got a caramel roll with nuts.

We continued at a relaxed pace, mostly because I was following feelings and had no idea where I was going. Yet somehow, it felt like I was headed in the right direction.

At Broadway and Penn, we ran across the intersection. It didn't seem anyone cared that pedestrians were trying to cross with the WALK light.

Still on Penn, we crossed Glenwood Avenue and entered the Bryn Mawr neighborhood. We crossed the bridge over some train tracks and Bassett Creek, more than forty blocks from home, and turned right on Chestnut. We went up a bit of a hill, past a sign company, and into Bassett Creek Park. We circled behind the tennis courts and the wildlife area with cattails as tall as me until we were following the train tracks alongside the creek. Frogs jumped toward the cattails as we approached. Insects madly chattered until we were within a step and would fall silent, only to begin again once we passed.

A sense of urgency grabbed me, and I walked faster. Two-thirds of the way across the park, the creek curved away from the train tracks, creating a small peninsula with a giant oak tree in the center. Its trunk was twisted and split, but green, healthy leaves populated the branches. Except for one broken branch on the lower right, probably damaged by the wind. It hung pointed at the ground, its leaves brown.

I stepped onto a rail, then a tie. As I crossed the second rail, John spoke for the first time I could remember since we left the Coffee Nook. "Daniels, where are you going?"

I didn't say anything, didn't stop. The peninsula was wet, soft, and mucky. My athletic shoes immediately took in water. A dark green and yellow ribbon snake about three feet long crossed in front of me then turned to follow the shore toward the tracks.

John picked carefully across the tracks, then ran to catch up to me. At the base of the oak tree was a pile of brush. A few oak branches, but mostly cattails, milkweed, goldenrod, and ragweed. Some tall grass. All things found along the tracks and creek.

I started pulling at the brush.

John grabbed my arm and tried to pull me away. "Daniels, stop. There could be something in there. Something with teeth and rabies."

I pushed him away and kept digging. A few inches down, I came across a light blue blanket. It was threadbare and dirty. The seam bound in satin had let go, leaving a few holes. I threw it aside and found a mattress.

John stood back a few feet, pale and paralyzed.

I dragged the mattress away and found Rachel Thompson.

CHAPTER SIXTEEN

Hanley, June 1998

Rose Ford laid her hand on the big man's forearm. "Hello, Richard. Thank you for coming."

"I'm sorry for your loss, ma'am," Hanley expressed.

"Thank you. Seems kind of senseless, doesn't it?"

"Yes, ma'am, it does," he remarked. "Can I ask what happened?"

Rose sighed. "They say he had a heart attack. I look out the window, and he's scraping the paint on the garage. It needed painting bad. Samuel was trying to keep busy, keep from thinking about our little girl." She wiped at her cheek. "It wasn't working. From the kitchen, I could see tears as he worked, reflecting light." She drew a deep breath. "The next time I look, he's lying on the ground. Wasn't nothing anybody could do."

"Did Samuel have a bad heart?" Hanley asked.

"No, but it was broken." She turned to face him. "Latisha was Samuel's world. He couldn't live without her."

"But he had you and LaNaya."

"He did." She smiled and looked away. "As much as he loved us, Latisha was his baby. He lived for her."

Hanley's eyebrows moved closer together, a crease forming between his eyes.

"I know what you're thinking," she claimed. "How can a parent love one more than another? Well, the truth is, LaNaya isn't his. She was a little girl when Samuel and I met and fell in love. He loved her, too. God, but he was good with her. But then Latisha came, and she owned him, heart and soul."

"I only talked with him the one time. The day he was installing the new lock."

"He finished it a few minutes after you left."

"I guess dinner had him motivated."

"It did. After dinner, he installed a new one in the back door, too. We're as secure as we've ever been."

"That day, he seemed okay. At least as okay as could be expected."

"I don't know how much you've lost, but grief is like waves. Some days the waves are small, some days they're whitecaps going right over your head." She shook hers. "You have good days, you have bad days. But grief, it's always there. You never forget."

"You're right. You don't," Hanley noted. "And that hardly seems right."

"You have to keep your faith, though. Have to believe it's all for a reason."

"The alternative, that it might be senseless, is unacceptable," Hanley stated.

"That it is," Rose agreed. "God wouldn't do that to us."

CHAPTER SEVENTEEN

<u>Daniels, August 2000</u>

Some of Rachel's clothes were gone, but I didn't see her skin. Didn't see what parts of her were exposed. A rope circled her neck, and her hands were tied. It was her eyes that again held my attention. Blue with flecks of gold, always sparkling, always smiling. Now they were dead, staring nowhere.

Except at me. Accusatory. Reminding me I was her protector and a failure. She'd been murdered and thrown away. The first casualty of my life, the one I would always remember. That would haunt me. A ghost of my own making?

"Oh, shit. Ah, fuck." It was the first time I remembered cursing other than "shit," which I only recalled saying once.

One of the advantages of knowing things, like after my nightmare knowing Rachel would not be found alive, was that I was difficult to surprise or scare. As a result, I didn't go into shock or panic or pee my pants. Instead, I thought,

Well, what are we going to do now? and *I better find John before something happens.*

When I'd uncovered Rachel, John had turned and ran like I probably should have but didn't. A scream tore from his throat. Then he fell silent. I took off after him, or at least in the direction I thought or felt he went. I ran behind the wildlife area and the tennis courts. I started behind the sign company, headed toward the Penn Avenue bridge. I was almost to a fence when I stopped. I don't know why. I slammed on the brakes at the edge of a large hole. In the process, I kicked some dirt and dust over the edge.

I looked down into the hole something had prevented me from falling into. John lay at the bottom, squinting through the dust. "I fell," he muttered.

"And I almost landed on top of you," I replied.

It wasn't a hole like utility workers would have dug. It was large and deeper than we were tall. It was wider at the bottom than at the top, making it almost impossible to claw your way to the top without falling back in.

I flopped down on my belly and reached down into the hole toward John. "Get up, and I'll pull you out."

His tears streaked the dust and dirt collected on his skin. "I can't."

I looked closer and realized it wasn't a hole. John had fallen into a trap. A stick, pointing up and sharpened like a spear, poked through John's lower left leg. Blood soaked his pants.

I swore again. John laughed, and I scowled at him. Maybe it was shock or panic, or maybe I was losing him. "What?" I asked.

"It sounds funny. You're not the type to swear."

86

"I am today."

I dropped into the hole and looked at the stick. Blood covered the tip that poked through his jeans. It was a few inches below his knee and close to the seam.

"Move your leg," I told him.

"What?" It came out as a whine.

"Just do it. Move your leg."

John moved his leg so his feet were closer together. Doing so didn't seem to cause him any pain, but the movement stopped when the stick pulled his jean leg tight. He moved his leg back the other way. He inhaled fast and hard between clenched teeth, kind of a backward whistle. Then he yelped and jerked the other way until his pant leg pulled tight again.

"Your leg hit the stick, didn't it?" I asked.

"Yeah," John reported. "And it hurt."

"I don't think the stick is through your leg," I told him. At least it was helpful in distracting him from why we were at the park.

"Then where is it?" he asked.

"I think you got lucky. I think you got a scratch. A big one, but only a scratch."

"Look at all the blood," he muttered. "You call that lucky?"

"Yeah."

"I'll probably get blood poisoning or lockjaw. I'm going to die."

"You're not going to die."

"They're going to cut my leg off," he insisted. "I'll be short like you."

"You won't be short. You only scratched one leg. You'll be lopsided. You'll walk in circles."

"I'll be the brunt of..." he began, then I joined in to finish. "Peg-leg jokes."

"Let's get you out of here so you can keep your leg." I grabbed his foot and began to lift his leg off the stick.

"Good idea," he agreed. But his muscles went rigid, and his fingers dug into the dirt beneath him.

I tried to keep his scratch away from the stick by pulling his jeans tight, but I heard another backward whistle and knew the wound had hit the stick. "I heard there are girls who like guys with scars," I remarked. "Maybe you'll have one. You can use it for show-and-tell." I couldn't tell how much he was bleeding, but I pulled off my button-down shirt and tied it around his leg. I knew we had to get him some help soon. Rachel, too.

"Can you stand?" I pulled John up, onto one foot, without letting him answer.

He put his foot down and leaned on his injured leg, then hit his head on the side of the hole where it narrowed. "I guess so," he replied. He brushed dirt from his hair, then used his middle finger to push up his glasses.

I still gripped his wrist. I wanted to be sure I had his attention. "We've got to get out of here," I declared, and he nodded. "We don't know who dug the trap. It could have been kids, you know. A bunch of sadistic assholes."

John *tsked* and shook his head.

"But it could have been whoever attacked Rachel, too. We don't want to get caught here, and we have to get someone to help her."

He let out a noise that reminded me of a wounded

werewolf in a movie we'd watched. Tears flowed again, and he wobbled a bit. I clamped on his wrist. If he went down again, he'd probably land on the spear and impale something important.

I kicked the stick until it broke and couldn't spear anything, then moved John to the middle of the hole and boosted him up. After he was out of the hole, he lay on his belly and reached down to pull me up. When I was above ground, I grabbed him, dragged him to his feet, and turned to lead him out of the field to Penn Avenue. From there, I hoped to find a cop, a payphone, or a neighbor willing to help.

Instead, we looked straight into the eyes of evil.

The tall, thin man had an olive complexion and dark, curly hair about two inches long. He was disheveled and dirty, carrying a pillowcase stuffed with probably everything he owned. Or maybe it was everything he had collected. One sleeve of a flannel shirt hung out. He was homeless or transient, or trying to give that impression.

It didn't matter. I knew what I was looking at.

His eyes softened, and the intense glare vanished. The color might have even changed. In a gentle voice, he asked, "Is there a problem?"

I pushed John in the opposite direction, away from the man. "It's him," I stated. "He did it. He killed Rachel."

CHAPTER EIGHTEEN

Latisha, June 1998

Latisha Ford walked up to the graveside and stood beside her father.

"I knew you were here, little girl," Samuel Ford told her.

"I've been here ever since," Latisha replied.

"Yeah, I know," he affirmed. "What have you been doing?"

"Waiting for my chance," Latisha noted. "Getting stronger."

"I've missed you so much."

They each wiped a tear and looked across the grave to where Rose and LaNaya sat, surrounded by friends and family. The cop who'd found Latisha stood in the back. "I feel the worst for your mama," Samuel remarked. "She's in so much pain. She misses you, too."

The minister finished a prayer, and the crowd stood. A couple of people Latisha didn't know hovered by her mama. The cop, Hanley, stayed close, too. Samuel turned and stepped away. "You coming, little girl?"

"No."

Rose and LaNaya held hands as they moved away. The minister took Rose's arm and supported her. Hanley walked next to LaNaya, his hands clasped behind his back.

"But it's time to go. Time to move on."

"Maybe for you. I'm not ready. I want to go home."

"You can't go home," Samuel told her. "C'mon, Latisha, let's go." He extended his hand and stepped toward her.

"No." Latisha started to run. "I'm not leaving. I'm going home."

A member of the funeral home staff lifted a bouquet from the center of Samuel's casket lid a moment before Latisha's hands landed there. She vaulted over the casket and across the open grave. She ran past the chairs her mama and sister had sat in and bolted across the cemetery, headed for the corner where she died.

"Please, little girl," Samuel whispered. "Please come with me." He looked at the back of his widow. "I don't know what to do."

Rose stopped at the car, then turned and looked at her husband's grave. "Be there when she's ready. Give her time," Rose replied. "I love you both."

"What was that, Mama?" LaNaya asked. "Did you say something?"

Rose shook her head. "I thought I heard your daddy's voice on the wind."

CHAPTER NINETEEN

<u>Daniels, August 2000</u>

We ran. In spite of John's hurt leg, we tore off behind the sign company, the tennis courts, and the wildlife area. Past Rachel and the oak tree as fast as we could. John, who normally wasn't a sprinter, for once took advantage of his long legs and kept up with me.

A path entered a wooded area on the far side of the park. I pointed, and we veered toward it. Once into the trees, the path sloped uphill. We slowed some and were breathing hard, but we kept going.

John and I came out of the trees behind a row of houses. We cut across the backyard of one and down its driveway, past a pair of rusting iron deer in the front yard, and onto Vincent Avenue, where we ran into two police cars in the middle of the street. The cops were holding one of those unexplainable conversations they always seemed to be having. Maybe they were providing a police presence. Maybe they wanted to make everybody nervous,

wondering what could be going on in their nice neighborhood.

We collided with the police cars. John lay across the
hood of the first one, panting at the bewildered policewoman behind the wheel. Her partner opened his door
and got out, his hand on his weapon.

I bounced off the first car, spun like a running back
changing directions, and ran around the front of the vehi-
cle, not stopping until I was between the two cars and their
open windows. Before any of the cops could say anything, I
blurted, "He's hurt, his sister is dead, and the guy who
killed her is back there in the park."

The two cops in the driver's seats got out of their cars.
The policewoman—Morse, according to her name tag—
calmly replied, "Say that again, but relax and slow down."
She was over six feet tall and looked muscular, one of those
policewomen you shouldn't mess with. The only things
soft about her were her gray, compassionate eyes and her
deep but still-gentle voice.

I pointed at John and addressed her partner. "It's his left
leg. I think it's a deep scratch. He'll probably need an
ambulance, at least a ride to the hospital."

The cop was stocky and shorter than Morse, with a
military-style buzz cut. His eyes reminded me of the
bullies I encountered at school. The ones I usually found
myself fighting on someone's behalf. His name tag said
Scheffler.

As he started to untie my partially blood-soaked shirt
from around John's leg, I turned to the other two, Morse
and a massive individual who, according to his tag, was
named Hanley. "Come with me. I'll explain as we go."

I started running the way John and I came, and they actually followed. As we were about to enter the trees, Morse called, "Wait. Tell us what's going on."

I stopped and drew a deep breath, trying to appear more winded than I actually was rather than exasperated. Neither of them appeared frustrated or breathing hard, only patient and concerned.

"Rachel Thompson has been missing for a couple of days. You've probably heard about her," I explained. They both nodded, and I continued. "John is her brother. We found her body. John got hurt running away in panic. Then we saw a guy down by the bridge. He's the one who kidnapped and murdered Rachel. I could tell by his eyes."

Hanley grabbed the microphone on his shoulder and pressed a button. "Scheffler, come in," he announced.

"This is Scheffler. Go."

"This is Hanley. If you think the kid can be moved, put him in your car and drive up to Penn. Get up on the bridge. Don't let anybody leave the park."

"Copy that," Scheffler declared. "On my way."

I turned and started through the trees, following the trail down the hill. We came out, and I led the two cops straight to the oak tree. The disheveled man I had seen, the one I knew killed Rachel, was beneath the tree. A piece of rope hung from his pocket. He was trying to cover Rachel's body with the mattress and brush I'd removed. He wore baggy painter's pants with a few spots of white and red and a black-and-red plaid flannel shirt. It was full of holes and hung open. Beneath it was a yellow tee shirt with more paint on it than his pants had and only a few holes.

When Hanley and Morse stopped him, their weapons

drawn, he looked at me. His dark eyes were again hard and cold. Even more than when I first saw him and knew he'd raped and murdered Rachel, that look convinced me bad guys and people who were just plain evil existed. The evil ones needed to be off the planet and on their way where they belonged. As long as it was Hell.

CHAPTER TWENTY

Latisha & Hanley, June 1998

Latisha fingered the deadbolt on the front door. "Daddy, you did it. You got the lock changed." She passed through the closed front door and found the house filled with people sitting wherever they could, balancing plates of food.

Rose Ford sat on the couch, dabbing her nose with a tissue. LaNaya huddled next to her. They were both wide-eyed, staring at LaNaya's hands, which lay in her lap. She seemed to be picking at something, trying to rip open a knuckle or pull out a splinter. Or maybe pull a finger off. Every once in a while, Rose would sigh, then pat LaNaya's leg or try to stop her hands from moving.

Latisha crossed through the room, stepping around the people. She touched the arm of the cop who found her and saw him shiver. She wondered why. Behind him, on the step, was her Siamese cat Mortimer. His gaze fixed on her, and he released a menacing tone. She shushed him. He fell silent but kept watching her as she moved through the room.

Pictures of Latisha and Samuel stood on easels behind the dining room table. A buffet lunch covered the top. "It looks like funeral food, Mama," Latisha commented. "You always hated funeral food." Latisha laughed. "You said it was too much Jell-O and Cool Whip and cheap lunch meat on bad bread."

The minister stood a few feet away, talking with a woman Latisha did not recognize. He said what a great tragedy it was that Rose and LaNaya had lost Latisha and Samuel so close together. When he stated, "But they're at peace and in a better place now," Latisha crossed the room and slapped his plate of food from his hands.

"Asshole," she spat. "You don't know shit."

The plate flew through the air and sprayed its contents across the dining room and the buffet. The plate, from Rose's good set of china, struck Samuel's picture in the forehead. It left a small blob of mayonnaise that made Samuel appear to have a pimple with a giant whitehead. Some salad-like thing made with Cool Whip, Jell-O, mandarin oranges, and cottage cheese slid down Latisha's picture, leaving a greasy smear across her cheek and settling against the frame.

"Oh, my," the minister remarked. "I have no idea how that happened. I thought I had a good grip on it."

Rose and LaNaya sat up on the edge of the couch. LaNaya watched the orange salad ooze past the frame and fall. Rose looked around the room as if she expected to see other things fly.

Latisha bumped into the cop as she ran past her mama

and up the stairs. With a miniature roar and a hiss, Mortimer fled before her into the bathroom. Rose turned to look as if she'd heard footsteps pass her and continue up the stairs. No one else seemed to notice.

Still, everyone glanced at the ceiling when the door to Latisha's bedroom slammed shut.

Richard Hanley stood near the staircase, nursing a glass of lemonade, wondering how long he should stay. He felt he had paid his respects, but Rose Ford's expectations and his own frustration at the department's inability to solve Latisha's murder weighed heavily on him. So did Samuel's death, which Rose was convinced happened because of Latisha's murder. He believed he didn't care what people thought of him. Yet he suspected everybody at the service and the lunch was looking at him, wondering when he was going to do his job.

A sudden chill overtook him, and his arm turned to gooseflesh. Behind him, the cat sitting on the steps made an unfriendly noise. Hanley looked at it, but its eyes were locked on something other than him.

He was sipping the lemonade when everything seemed to slow down. The plate flew from the minister's hands, scattering its contents until it hit Samuel's picture and fell.

Seconds later, Hanley felt another chill and what might have been a bump if somebody were there. The cat yowled, hissed, and ran up the stairs. When an upstairs door slammed shut, his hand moved toward the weapon he wasn't carrying.

It hadn't been the cat slamming the door.

Hanley's ears worked overtime as he finished his lemonade, tossed the empty plastic cup into a wastebasket, and wandered upstairs. He wondered why he hadn't brought his weapon. He was in his civilian clothes, attending a funeral. He shouldn't have needed it. Yet here he was, searching a house, unarmed.

Two bedrooms had to belong to Mrs. Ford and LaNaya. They were neat and quiet. So was a third room, which held a desk, a computer, and a sewing machine.

He peeked into the bathroom. The cat hid underneath the toilet tank, shaking.

A fourth door stood at the end of the hall, the south-west corner of the house. Hanley opened the closed door and stepped into the room. This one had to belong to Latisha. It was unoccupied, with no open windows or strong breezes that would have explained the door slamming.

He came back downstairs to find one of Rose's sisters and a friend had cleaned up the mess from the flying food. The incident had been a mood-breaker, though. Within minutes, people started to leave. Hanley lined up with a group heading out, and Rose wrapped him in a hug. "If you or LaNaya need anything, you call me," he told her. "Okay?"

Rose nodded. "Just find my baby's killer," she responded. "I know you can."

"I'll keep on it," Hanley promised. "We'll get him."

Latisha looked around her bedroom. The only thing different since the last time she had been here was the bed being made. Rose had taught her daughters to keep their rooms neat, but she had never been able to convince Latisha that a neat room included a made bed.

She watched the cop open the door she had slammed. When he left, she pressed the play button on her Sony Walkman CD player that lay on the headboard. "God Bless the Child" by Billie Holiday came through the headphone's tiny speakers. She slipped them on, sang along, and wondered if Billie was right. If God did bless the children who got their own. Did that somehow mean she was supposed to get her killer? If only she'd get the chance.

CHAPTER TWENTY-ONE

<u>Daniels, August 2000</u>

Officers Hanley and Morse holstered their weapons after they had cuffed the guy. They kept him lying on the ground until additional cops arrived. It looked as if most of the Minneapolis Police force came, along with a few from the Hennepin County Sheriff's Department and the Minnesota Bureau of Criminal Apprehension.

I looked at the bridge in time to see John move from the police car to one of the two ambulances that had arrived.

Crime scene people came, put up tape, took pictures, and searched.

Scheffler and another cop took the guy up to a squad car sitting on Chestnut, stuffed him in the backseat, then stood near the car. I still stood where I'd been when Morse and Hanley grabbed him. I wanted to check on John, but I didn't want to leave Rachel. She won, so I stayed close to where she lay. I didn't look in her direction, though. I turned toward Chestnut and stared at her killer's silhouette in the back seat of the car.

Could he feel me stare? Did he feel me thinking about blood vessels in his head breaking or his intestines wrapping themselves into a knot? I wished my gift was telekinesis so I could reach out with my mind, grab his heart with my cold thoughts, and subject him to a painful death. Slowly squeeze the life out of him. No such luck, though.

Hanley wandered off through the trees, and Morse arrived next to me. "How are you doing?" she asked.

"Okay, I guess," I replied. "How about you?"

The corner of her mouth went up a bit. "I'm fine, thank you." She turned to see what I was staring at. "I'm not very good at scenes like this," she admitted.

"Really? You don't see too much, get immune?" I asked.

"No, we don't," she answered. "We're here because somebody lost a daughter. Every story is different. So is everybody's pain. But in every story, someone always loses somebody or something. So you care. You try to help when you can. You try not to let it make you nuts." She stared at me for a long second. "Why am I telling you this? You don't need to hear it. You're a kid who lost a friend. I'm sorry."

"It's okay," I assured her. "I asked, you needed to talk, and I'm here to listen and learn."

"Does everybody open to you like this?" Morse asked.

"I don't know. I never noticed."

"I never asked your name," she realized.

"Jacob Daniels. Everybody calls me Daniels."

"Do you know John and Rachel pretty well?"

"Yeah, we're friends. We hang out quite a bit."

"He's going to need you now more than ever," she advised.

"Probably," I agreed. "But he'll be okay."

"You seem pretty sure about that."

I shrugged. "Funny feeling. Sometimes you just know things about people."

Hanley pulled his car onto Chestnut and parked across the street from the car holding Rachel's killer. He walked to where Morse and I waited. "What's your name, kid?"

"Daniels."

"Okay, Daniels, what can you tell us?"

"John and I went searching for Rachel and ended up here. I uncovered her body, and John ran off screaming and fell into a trap. That's where his leg got hurt."

"Trap?" Morse asked. "What kind of trap?"

"It's a big hole. Deeper than we are tall, wide at the bottom, with a spear stuck in the ground and pointed up. That's what sliced John. It's behind the building, almost to the bridge. I can show you."

"In a few minutes," Hanley acknowledged. "Please continue with your story."

Both cops had notebooks and pens in their hands, but their gazes were locked on me.

"I got John out of the hole, and we turned and saw the guy you caught, and I knew he was the one who killed Rachel. We ran out of the park, trying to get away from him and find some help, and we found you."

"What did you see when you uncovered the…" Hanley stopped. "When you found Rachel?"

"Her hands were tied, and she had a rope around her neck."

"There isn't a rope around her neck," Hanley pointed out.

"It's in his pocket," I declared. "Or was. I saw it when we came back to the park. I think that's how he killed her."

Hanley walked away, talked with a woman in a light jacket marked Police Lab, then spoke on his radio for a minute. "What else did you see?" he asked when he came back.

"I don't know. Some of her clothes were missing, but I don't know what. It didn't register." I cleared my throat and sniffed. "Once I got past the ropes, I really only saw her eyes. I knew she was dead, and I couldn't help her anymore."

"You helped by finding her," Morse stated. "And by leading us to the man who may have killed her."

"Oh, he did it. I know it."

"How do you know?" Hanley asked.

"Funny feeling," I noted. "I just know."

Hanley's radio crackled, and he walked away. When he came back, he announced, "They found your trap. How did it look when you left it?"

"You should find some of John's blood in the dirt and on the spear, which I kicked until it broke so we wouldn't fall on it when we climbed out. I don't remember seeing anything else in the hole. No dead animals or anything, so I don't know how long it had been there."

"They're still checking it out," Hanley reported. "Also, the ambulance is ready to take John to the hospital. He says he's fine and wants to stay here." He looked at Morse. "Maybe you and Daniels should ride with him, get him to go." Morse nodded, and Hanley continued. "Scheffler will meet you there. I'll go get the parents."

She started to walk away from where we stood. I hesitated. "You can help Rachel more by talking with us later," Morse told me. "Right now, you need to help John. Get him to the hospital and get him patched up."

"Yeah, I suppose." I followed Morse, but Hanley remained where we had been, except he turned to face where Rachel still lay.

Morse realized I was staring at Rachel's killer again. "You should probably watch where you're going."

"I'm fine," I insisted. "I know where to step."

"Have you seen this guy before?" she asked.

"Nope."

"So you don't know him or recognize him from somewhere?" Morse asked.

"No."

"Then how do you know he did it?" she asked.

"Ask John," I suggested. "He'll tell you."

CHAPTER TWENTY-TWO

Officer Morse and I left the park and headed up Chestnut toward Penn, where the ambulance sat on the bridge. I climbed in the open door and got in the back. Morse followed, and we each took a bench seat. One paramedic climbed in with us while the other sat behind the steering wheel.

John sat on the gurney, his leg elevated and stretched out. "I can't leave Rachel."

"We need to get you patched up," I told him.

"I'm plenty patched. The bleeding has probably stopped, and my leg looks like a mummy," John claimed. "I can't leave Rachel."

"I was sure you were going to be this way. I told Officer Morse to give you something to make you unconscious and send you to the hospital."

"You did not."

"You know I did," I countered, and Morse nodded. "Instead, she said we should go along with you, make sure you were okay, talk about stuff. Then we can go back to helping Rachel."

"Yeah, I guess," John conceded. "We'll have to take care of my mom and dad, too."

The ambulance rumbled to life and began to roll up the street.

"Officer Hanley is picking them up," Morse explained. "They'll meet us at the hospital. Your parents, too, Daniels."

"It's only my mom, but she'll want to be there."

"Tell me, John," Morse continued. "How did you find Rachel?"

"Shouldn't you question us separately?" I asked.

"I don't know," she stated. "Should I? Are you guilty of something?"

"No. I figured you'd compare our stories, make sure we aren't up to something."

"I don't believe you two are up to anything," Morse declared. "I only want to know how you found her. I've heard your story, and now I'm going to hear his. Since yours is full of holes, I'll compare them. Now, you're going to sit quiet, and John is going to tell me."

"Okay. I'm just trying to help."

"Uh-huh," John muttered.

"John, how did you two find Rachel?" Morse asked. "You're a long way from home."

"We did go a long way," John agreed. "I have no idea where we actually ended up. I'm not sure I've even been through this neighborhood. It certainly isn't on any of our usual routes. I was only following."

"How did you get there?"

"We walked."

"Who were you following?" Morse asked.

"Daniels."

"Who was he following?"

"No one," John declared.

"Then how *did* he know where he was going?"

"He's psychic."

"Really?" she asked. Her eyebrows went up, and she leaned forward.

"He'll tell you he isn't, but he is," John assured her. "He's passed all of my tests."

"How many tests have you subjected your friend to?"

"Oh, lots. I made up some, and some I read about," he explained. "By definition and objective, he passed them all."

"Wow," Morse remarked. "We'll come back to the tests."

"Okay. I can show you my notes. They're very well documented."

"I'm sure they are." She gave him a quick smile. "Tell me about your day. What did you do?" Morse asked. "Tell me all of it."

"Daniels came over, woke me up, and said he dreamed about Rachel. I said it was a sign that he could find her. I got dressed, he started walking, I followed, and he led us right to her."

"Then why didn't he find her earlier?"

"I don't know. I know he tried," John insisted. "I'm sure there's a connection between his dream and his ability to find her. Sometimes he knows things, especially when he first meets someone, but a lot of times, he has to be stressed. Like scared or tired from having nightmares. Then his ability kicks in, and he can find things."

"How do I put this in my report?" Morse asked.

"Do any of the people who read your reports believe in psychics?" John asked.

"I don't know. That's not something we talk about very often."

"You have to follow too many rules," I pointed out. "You need things to be rational and orderly. What John told you doesn't fit into that."

"How do you know I don't believe in ESP?" Morse asked.

I shrugged. "I don't. I was making a generalization. Adults need to behave rationally. I'm sure it's worse for those of you who work in law enforcement. So even if you do believe, you're not going to advertise it."

Morse laughed. "You're right, and I'm not going to wander around asking who does and doesn't," she confessed. "Though the DA might have to when he tries to find a jury based on your story."

"So maybe you should build a solid case using evidence and not rely on my story," I suggested. "Although the TV people should like my version better."

The ambulance pulled into the garage at North Memorial Medical Center in Robbinsdale and backed up to an automatic entrance. The paramedic who'd driven got out, circled to the back, and opened the rear doors.

Morse and I followed the paramedics as they pushed John into the hospital on the gurney. They wheeled him down the hall and into a room created by two solid walls and two curtains. A bed was backed against the wall. A computer console stood beside it with half a dozen cords plugged into the wall, a few to the bed, and more going around the bed to electronic gadgets on a cart.

John looked embarrassed as he lay on the gurney. "I can walk, you know."

"Not according to hospital regulations, you can't," the paramedic closest to his head announced. "At least, not while you're with us."

"You're here because you already fell once today," I stated. "They're not going to risk it happening again."

"I don't think I'll find any giant holes in the hospital floor to fall into."

"One could open up and try to swallow you. Just enjoy the ride."

"Yeah, that way, it has to be a hole big enough to swallow all of us. I'm safer here."

"Exactly."

"You guys watch too much TV," Morse interrupted.

"That's not possible," John rejoined.

The paramedics pushed the gurney against the bed, then picked up John and the sheet he was lying on and moved them to the bed. One pushed the gurney out of the room and headed back down the hallway. The other made some notations on a clipboard, then stated, "Take it easy, kid," and left, too.

Morse stood near the door and looked down the hallway into the next room, then back to me and John. "Are you guys okay?" she asked. John shrugged, and I nodded. "I'm going to check in with the nurses and wait for my partner to show up," she told us.

"Okay," I replied. "We're kind of tired, so I think we'll wait here until someone says we can leave."

"I'm sure the doctor will be in soon to check you out. After all, they don't want you here anymore than you want to be," she stated. "Officer Hanley and your parents should be here soon, too. I'm sure they'll be anxious to take you home."

"We'll be ready," I declared.

"Thank you, Officer," John added. He turned his head toward the wall, but I thought I saw a couple of tears.

Morse nodded. "I'll check back with you," she promised and left.

John continued to face the wall. I didn't have to be psychic to know his thoughts. I perched in a chair near the foot of the bed and read a couple of pamphlets I found near the computer. One was about Lyme disease, the other on how to recognize the symptoms of a stroke. Neither was very exciting, but it gave me something to do.

A nurse came in, smiled at me, and quietly talked to John. She was about my mom's size, bigger than me but not very big, and probably in her twenties. Her wavy brown, highlighted hair was about two inches long. Balloons and flowers decorated the top of her scrubs. Some noise outside the room kept me from hearing what she and John whispered about, but I guessed he answered some questions since the conversation seemed to go back and forth. She took his temperature with a little gauge she held up to his ear, checked his blood pressure, then unwound the bandage from his leg.

I stood and stepped up to the bed. "Is it going to fall off?" I asked.

"Why would you think that?" she asked.

"Will you need to amputate?" I dragged my finger across my throat like I was slicing it open. "Just below the chin, so he's not too short."

"Of course not. How can you..." She stopped when John started laughing. "Is this how you deal with pain and stress?" she asked with a smile. "I could fake a chart saying you had your jaw broken and get your mouth wired shut."

"Really?" John asked. "You're talking about *his* mouth, right?"

"So far, yeah,"

"That would be so cool," he replied. "Let's do it."

A tall, dark-haired doctor wearing a lab coat over a set of scrubs walked in. "Do what?" he asked.

"They'd like each other's mouths wired shut," the nurse stated as she walked out of the room.

"I'm afraid we can't do that," the doctor noted. "Patients have to be able to eat to get out of here. We can only install zippers."

"That would work," John replied. "I could glue his zipper shut at home."

"I'm Doctor Erickson." He pulled a stool up to the bed and looked John in the eye. "I'm going to patch you up." John met his gaze even as he shifted his head a bit and changed the angle. "Sounds like you've had quite a day. I'm really sorry about your sister."

"Thank you." He began to examine the blanket lying next to him.

"It's good that they found her," the doctor offered. "At least we know for sure."

"He found her," John corrected.

"I beg your pardon?" the doctor asked.

"Daniels found her. "It wasn't the police or anybody else. He found her."

Doctor Erickson looked at me. His eyebrows went up a bit. "Wow. That's great. Way to go."

"John was with me, too," I pointed out.

"And I heard they caught the guy," the doctor mentioned.

"Yeah, they did," John stated. "Too bad he didn't resist arrest. It could all be over."

Doctor Erickson cleared his throat. "Let's look at your leg." He got off the chair, leaned over the bed, and straightened John's leg. "Looks like a scrape. There really isn't anything I can sew or glue."

"You use glue?" I asked.

"Yeah," Dr. Erickson confirmed. "It's kind of like Super Glue, but it gets absorbed into the body." He twisted John's leg so it rolled at the hip, and he could get a better look toward the back. "The bleeding has stopped, and it's already beginning to scab. I think a tetanus shot and an antibiotic are in order. Then we'll wrap it. You keep it clean, protect it, and I think you'll heal just fine."

"Will it leave a scar?" John asked.

"Probably."

"Girls like scars," I proclaimed.

"Is that true?" John asked.

"I don't know," Dr. Erickson remarked as the nurse entered the room. "Let's ask. Nurse Conger, is it true women like men with scars?"

"Depends on the guy." She entered some information into the computer without looking at us. "My boyfriend's skin is flawless and smooth as a baby's butt, and I like it." She turned away from the computer and looked at John. "You, however. I think it will enhance your ruggedness, your sense of mystery. It's going to work for you." When she looked into his eyes and smiled at him, I thought he was going to melt.

"Wow," Dr. Erickson commented. "Makes me want to get a scar." He laughed, and after Nurse Conger smiled again and left the room, he turned to John. "You'll be fine. I'll be back in a little while to wrap your leg and give you the shots. We'll see if we can't get you out of here soon." He rapped his knuckles on the bed railing and left.

After we were alone and the room was quiet, John sighed. "Yeah, we found her and they caught him and maybe I'll be fine, but I never get to see my sister again." Tears pooled along the bottom of his lenses, reached the corner of his dark frames, and fell to the bed.

"Maybe not," I suggested. "You and I both believe that spirits are all around us."

"Do you think we'll see her again?"

"I don't know, but I'm sure she's watching us. Or at least you. You were her favorite brother, after all."

"I was her only brother, asshole."

"Okay, so maybe you were short on competition, but you were still her favorite."

"I suppose." He half-flopped on the bed so he could turn away from me while trying not to move his leg.

"I'm going to miss her, too," I declared. "She was the best sister we both could have had."

Without turning back to face me, he released a chuckle, then sniffled. His hand moved up to his face and rubbed his eyes.

Mr. and Mrs. Thompson came into the room, followed by my mom. They stopped inside the curtain and looked at us. Mr. Thompson was the first to speak. "The police came to the house. They said you had gotten hurt, and they brought us here. How did you get hurt?"

John rolled over to face them. "Finding Rachel," he replied. The tears began to flow freely.

"Where were you looking for Rachel that you could get hurt?" Mrs. Thompson asked.

"We weren't looking for Rachel," John countered. "We found her."

"I don't understand. What are you saying?" Mrs. Thompson asked.

Mom looked at me, the question obvious in her expression. I nodded. She stepped toward me and gestured me up with her finger. I stood, and she wrapped me in her arms.

Morse and Hanley appeared at the curtain. Morse looked at John's parents. "Mr. and Mrs. Thompson?" They turned toward her, and Morse regarded my mom. "Mrs. Daniels?" Mom nodded and released me. "I'm Linda Morse. You met Officer Hanley when he picked you up. I'm sorry we had to meet like this."

"I don't understand what's going on," Mr. Thompson declared. "How did John get hurt? What's he saying about finding Rachel?"

"Well, it appears John and Daniels went for a long walk and found Rachel. In a panic, John ran, fell, and got speared by a stick."

"It's only a scrape," John explained. The tears had disappeared. "But it'll leave a scar." He turned his leg so everyone could see his wound.

"Where's Rachel?" Mrs. Thompson asked. "Is she okay?"

"I'm afraid not," Morse admitted.

"She's dead, Mom," John announced. "Somebody killed Rachel."

He started to cry again

Mr. Thompson stood there, his head slowly shaking. Mrs. Thompson began to quiver, starting with her lower lip and spreading to her entire body. She fell toward John, and Mr. Thompson followed a step later, sweeping them into a group hug.

Mom put an arm around me and whispered, "Walk with me." She steered me out of the room. "Let's give them some time. Go get something to drink." We walked about twenty feet down the hall and turned the corner. Mom stepped in front of me and wrapped her arms tightly around me. I returned the hug until my arms began to ache.

She held my shoulders and stared into my eyes. "You can imagine what I was thinking when I find your note, get to the Thompsons', and you and John are gone and no one knows where you went. Then, a few hours later, not minutes but hours, a police officer shows up and asks us all to come with him."

"I can imagine," I stated. "You know where we went, though."

"Specifics are nice sometimes."

"I had nothing specific to share."

She drew a deep breath. "I don't really need to tell you what I'm thinking, do I?"

I shook my head.

"There's really no point in getting mad and yelling at you, is there?"

"I only wanted to help," I told her. "I had to try."

"I know."

She turned and hooked her elbow in mine, and we continued down the hall. We strolled a long hallway, took the elevator to the basement, and wandered into the vending area of the cafeteria without saying another word. Mom dug change from her purse, fed it into one of the machines, and I hit a button. Coca-Cola Classic in a plastic bottle banged through the little door. Mom fed the machine more change. When I looked at her, she commented, "John will need something." I hit the button for a Sprite.

As we walked out of the cafeteria, she took my Coke, twisted open the top, and gulped a big drink. She carried it to the elevator and sipped again, then screwed the cap back on and handed it to me.

We didn't talk through the remainder of the trip back to John's room.

Morse and Hanley waited outside the curtain. The doctor emerged and gave us a smile.

"Mrs. Daniels," Morse stated. "We'd like to talk with you and the Thompsons for a bit."

"Of course," Mom agreed.

We walked into the room. John's leg had been wrapped. Mr. Thompson stood near the foot of the bed. His pallor and lack of movement reminded me of a zombie. Mrs. Thompson stood near the head, her hand resting on John's cheek.

"Helen, Peter. The police would like to talk with us," Mom advised. "Daniels can hang here with John, and we can go somewhere else and answer their questions. Maybe get a few of ours answered, too."

Mr. Thompson drifted out, looking even more zombie-like when he moved. Mom put an arm around Mrs. Thompson and led her away. She seemed to not want to leave John. Her arm stretched back toward him as they left.

When the adults were gone, John and I stared at each other for a moment. I handed him the Sprite and sat in the chair I had been using earlier.

Nurse Conger pushed the curtains open and came into the room. She asked John if he felt nauseous and how much pain he had, then took his temperature, blood pressure, and pulse. She entered the information into the computer.

With the curtain back, I noticed Officer Scheffler standing nearby, staying out of the way and looking grumpy.

John and I sat silent for a while. Then he stated, "Nothing's going to be the same, is it?"

"I guess not," I replied.

We returned to silence.

Someone pushed a kid in a wheelchair past the opening in the curtains and deeper into the emergency room. He was about our age. He was pale and thin, his head hanging. Five people followed behind the chair, looking broken and frantic. Something told me his problems were heading toward a final resolution. And not a positive one.

Mom, Hanley, and Morse reappeared and stood outside the room, talking quietly. Occasionally, one of them would smile. They seemed to take turns. They shook hands, the police walked away, and Mom came into the room.

"I think the police are done with us," she mentioned. "Your parents are talking with the people from the hospital. They should be here soon." She pulled me to my feet, stood me in the middle of the room, and began an inspection. "I'm impressed with your new friends."

Friends? We were hanging with the police. Could they be friends? "What are you looking for?" I asked.

"Just checking."

"Didn't you do that when you hugged me a few minutes ago?" I asked.

"Yeah, but I need to be sure."

"I'm fine," I assured her. "The medical experts didn't miss anything."

"Officers Hanley and Morse are very professional and caring," Mom remarked. "It will be good to have them on your side."

I looked at John. He appeared as confused as I was. "On our sides for what?" I asked.

"You never know," she declared. "You never know when you'll need a friend like them." Inspection complete, she stepped in front of John and took his hands. "I'm so sorry about Rachel. It must be horrible." A smile flickered across her lips. "On the other hand, I'm glad it was you two who found her. She knew you cared and were trying."

Mom released John's hands, and they both wiped away tears. She looked at me. "I know you think you're tough and mature, but you two should not be off finding bodies. Even if it is Rachel. You need to be more careful. This could have gone much worse than it did." I shook my head, and she sighed before continuing. "Don't tell me what you know or think you know, or what you think I know. I don't care. You two need to be more careful."

CHAPTER TWENTY-THREE

<u>Hanley, June 1998</u>

Hanley went to the downtown headquarters of the Minneapolis Police Department and made his way to the Violent Crimes Division. He found Detective Whitehead at the coffee machine, adding lots of sugar to a cup that, based on the color, already had lots of creamer. Whitehead was a white male in his late fifties. His buzz-cut gray hair needed a touchup. He slouched and was thickening in the middle. Hanley wondered if he could run down a perp if he needed to.

"Hey, Rich," Whitehead greeted. "Can I buy you a cup?"

Hanley looked at the setup. The force provided the coffee. You didn't even have to pitch in some change like you did at the Northside Precinct, where he usually worked. "No, thanks," he replied. "I'm not much of a coffee drinker."

"I am, as long as it doesn't taste like coffee." Whitehead sipped his cup, then picked up the sugar again. "What brings you down here?"

"I was at Samuel Ford's memorial," Hanley answered.

"Who?" Whitehead asked.

"Latisha Ford's father. I couldn't help thinking about her. Thought I should see how it's going, ask if there is anything I can do to help."

"Latisha Ford," Whitehead mused. "Oh yeah, you found her body. Up in Camden."

"Yeah," Hanley confirmed. "How's it going?"

"That one is frustrating," Whitehead admitted. "Went cold in a hurry. Not a lot of physical evidence. A bit of DNA from the rope on her neck, but no match to anything in the system. He wore a condom. Not that it matters since we got a sample from the rope. No murders in North Minneapolis have matching MOs. The family and friends all checked out, and there weren't any registered sex offenders in the area at the time. Like I said, cold."

"But we're still working it?" Hanley asked.

"Yeah, but the guy's a ghost," Whitehead insisted. "Until we get a tip or he screws up, he's going to stay out there. With the rate people are killing each other, we're getting all we can off the streets, but it isn't enough. We could use some help on them, too."

"I'll keep talking to everyone I know," Hanley promised. "But if there's anything, especially on the Ford case, I'd like to be involved."

"Thanks, Rich," Whitehead told him. "We appreciate it. We'll keep it in mind."

Hanley left Whitehead as he slipped his coffee cup into the microwave. When in the elevator and alone, Hanley muttered, "What the fuck have you been doing? And you call yourselves detectives."

CHAPTER TWENTY-FOUR

Daniels, August 2000

It was hot and humid the afternoon they had a service for Rachel and buried an urn. They called what was left of her the cremains. It didn't sound right.

Mom and I were at the church early with John and his parents. We had spent most of the last few days with them as family and friends came to visit. It really seemed as if Mom played host and tried to keep them together. I hung out with John. We found it impossible to do much more than mope.

Mom didn't push me to wear a suit, which was fine. John looked miserable in his. Rachel had helped him pick it out for a wedding the Thompsons had attended earlier in the year. The sleeves and pants already looked a little short, but John said Rachel would have insisted he wear it so she could tell him he looked like the funeral director's assistant. At the wedding, she had called him Lurch.

I told him he looked more like a math teacher. Math was his least favorite class, the subject he was least likely to teach. He used his middle finger to push his glasses up his nose and made sure I saw it.

Before the doors opened to the public, I stood in the front of the church, near the urn surrounded by flowers, and looked at some of the picture boards that John, Mrs. Thompson, and Mom had put together the night before. I mostly watched and listened as Mrs. Thompson recalled where the picture was taken and why.

While we had sat at the dining room table, working on the displays, Mr. Thompson picked up two pictures and carried them onto the front porch. One was of Rachel as a baby. The other was her last school picture. I thought it was one of her best. My copy was in my collection at home. Mr. Thompson sat on the top step, cradled the pictures against his chest, and rocked. I couldn't tell from my angle, but I suspected he cried. I know I wanted to just watching him.

The pictures on the display board I stared at were recent ones, taken by friends and collected by Rachel. Her mom had found them in a photo album on the shelf above Rachel's desk. Boyfriends weren't included unless they were part of a group. Most of the pictures were of Rachel and her friends being squirrelly. Or making attempts at being glamorous. Rachel came the closest to pulling it off.

Mrs. Thompson sent John out of the chapel, then came to the front and stood next to me. "I want to thank you for being John and Rachel's friend," she told me.

"You're welcome," I replied. "I've enjoyed being their friend."

"You've been a part of our family for a long time now.

Even Rachel admitted how much she enjoyed having you around."

"Wow, I'm honored. That's really nice to hear. It means a lot to me."

She put an arm around my shoulders. "And thank you for finding my daughter for me."

I turned to face her. "I'm sorry I couldn't do it sooner."

"It was nothing you could control. I learned that a long time ago, when I started…" She made quotation marks in the air with her fingers. "Knowing things." She looked around, then backed up to a chair in the front row. I followed and sat next to her. "That's the hardest part in all this. Knowing that no matter how hard we may try, we can't change some things. They are inevitable." Her hands lay in her lap, clenched so tight they were turning red. As if the blood were pooling in her fingertips. "I knew from the moment I touched the doorknob that I'd lost my Rachel."

"I understand what you're telling me, and I know you've had more experience with knowing things," I admitted. "But I cannot yet accept I can't make a difference. I choose to believe the messages are open to interpretation. I choose to believe that nothing is set. That I can still make a difference and help somebody."

"But we knew, and we couldn't save Rachel."

"And I'm not handling that very well at all. I can't accept it as reality, even though I know it's true. So in the future, I have to try. Have to not let it happen again."

"What if I'm right, and you can't save everybody?" she asked.

"I still have to try. I have to believe I can," I insisted. "Otherwise, why was I given this ability?"

"Well, you keep that faith. You keep trying," Mrs. Thompson stated. "Maybe you can make a difference. I know I haven't been able to, and it about drives me crazy." She reached into a pocket, pulled out a mangled tissue, and wiped at her eyes. "I'm sorry. I shouldn't be saying these things to you. You're too young to worry about adult stuff."

"It's okay," I remarked. "It's probably better me than John. I understand a little better since I'm the way I am, too."

She reached out and hugged me. "Thank you."

"Any time," I declared.

"I'm going to tell your mom some of this, too. Especially the thanks and the family parts. You've both been wonderful."

"It's mostly her. She teaches me something every day. But thank you."

Her hug tightened almost to the point of crushing before she stood and wandered to the back of the chapel.

———

Rachel's visitation and funeral service had been crowded. The church lacked air movement, as if they had sucked the air out and blocked the breeze. An endless parade of people loved Rachel and her family. Most of them, I had never seen before.

The graveside service was long and sweaty. The Thompson family plot was in an area devoid of trees. The little awning beside the grave didn't provide nearly enough shade, and the sun baked us. By the time we left, a few shoulders and bald heads had begun to redden. Only the crowd of people waving their hands or any paper they carried generated any breeze.

When we returned to the church for lunch, at least we were in the basement, where it was a few degrees cooler.

According to my mom, Mrs. Thompson was losing weight so fast she had nothing that fit. Her new dress was light blue, and every time somebody complimented her, she told them it was Rachel's favorite color. By this time, her eyes were red and swollen, her nose rubbed raw, her complexion pasty. Still, she managed a smile for everyone who approached her.

John stayed close to his mother, who introduced him to everyone. He managed to smile and be gracious. She sent him on errands a few times, and I would go along. So would our friend Warren Marsh who, like me, stayed close in case John needed us.

"I don't know why I have to meet these people," John complained. This time, we were walking to the Thompsons' car for the extra pair of shoes his mother had brought. John hurried along, his long legs propelling him quickly between the parked cars. "I don't know them, will probably never see them again, and I'm not even convinced they know Rachel." He stopped walking and turned to face us as we caught up to him. "Why do we do all this funeral crap, anyhow? Rachel's dead. She doesn't care."

"Mom says we do it for the survivors, not the deceased," I replied.

"Yeah," Warren added. "It's supposed to help bring closure. I'm not sure how dredging up memories or hearing new stories about a person closes anything, though. I would think it keeps them alive more, even though they're gone."

John shook his head. "All this reminds me that I miss Rachel. It hurts."

"Maybe we need them to stay alive longer," I suggested. "At least until we're ready to deal with their absence." I shrugged. "Maybe it lets us know them better."

"Maybe it's all bullshit," John proclaimed. "Promise me you'll spare my dead ass all this crap."

"We'll try," Warren answered.

"But your mom won't be happy," I pointed out.

"I don't know that Mom, Dad, or I will ever be happy again," John stated. Then he turned and ran to the car. After John was out of earshot, Warren told me, "I feel guilty about not being here to help with the search."

Warren had found John and me during elementary school, not long after John and I started hanging together. We were almost the Three Musketeers. Or, as Rachel would have insisted, the Three Stooges.

"It was really nice of your parents to cut your vacation short so you could be here," I noted.

Warren nodded. "Mom and Dad have always liked the Thompsons. It wasn't hard to convince them once we heard." His mouth moved around like he was chewing something or biting the inside of his cheek. "And Rachel, man, she was the best." Warren had never tried to hide his appreciation of John's sister. Not like I had.

"How did you hear?" I asked.

"Your mom called. Evidently, all of our parents talk regularly. Mine had left contact information with your mom before we went."

"I'm glad she did."

John strolled back, shoes in hand, and we walked back into the church as slowly and silently as possible.

Mr. Thompson didn't manage a smile for anybody. If he wasn't looking at someone's face, he was staring off into space. During the visitation and the lunch after the graveside service, he spent most of the time standing near the poster boards covered with pictures. One close-up showed Rachel from the middle of her forehead to her chin, her smile broad, her eyes sparkling. Mr. Thompson kept touching it as if he were beeping her nose. The pictures he had carried to the porch the night before were in his shirt pocket.

I was surprised at how many pictures I was in. Evidently, I spent more time involved in Thompson family activities than I realized. The number of pictures where I was closer to Rachel than John was disturbed me. They looked almost as if someone had pointed the camera, and she pulled me between them. I wasn't the only one who noticed it. A few people pointed at my face in some picture or another and asked, "Who is this? He isn't a boyfriend, is he?"

When it was only Warren and me looking at the pictures, he commented, "Daniels, it was nice of you to let John into the pictures of you and your sister. I never did believe those two were related." He scanned the boards again. "How come I'm not in any? I had to have been there at least once when a camera was out."

"I'm sure she deleted or tossed any pictures that included you," I retorted. "I know I have."

Mom led the ladies who provided the lunch. They had

managed to get quite a few of Rachel's favorites. Fried chicken, potato salad, three different kinds of chips, M&M's. I wondered how she kept thin and pimple-free. I ate very little and still came away feeling greasy.

As we cleaned up after lunch, Warren noted, "The police were crawling all over the place, weren't they?"

"I saw Morse and Hanley," John confirmed. "Were there others?"

"Lots of them. You'd think they were expecting her killer to show up. But they already have him, don't they?"

"They got the right one," I insisted. "I think they were showing their support. They're not looking for anyone else."

"Unless they were looking for you," Warren mentioned.

"They weren't looking for me," I insisted.

"How do you know?" Warren asked.

"They've already checked me out. Besides, they know where to find me."

"Maybe they were looking for the girls playing in the cemetery," John remarked.

"What girls?" Warren wondered.

"Yeah," I agreed. "I didn't see any girls who weren't attending the funeral. Certainly none off playing."

"There were a few of them," John claimed. "The way they'd disappear and pop back up, I thought they were playing hide-and-seek."

"Describe them," Warren urged.

John paused to think. "They were around our age. Some a bit older, some a bit younger. They weren't dressed for a funeral. A few were kind of cute."

"Hmm. I guess I missed them," I noted. "Maybe I was

facing the wrong way."

"Maybe they were really good at hiding," Warren suggested. "Because you know how I can always find a cute girl."

"You have to find them because after they meet you the first time, they hide," I countered.

John smirked. "And if they get to know you, Daniels and I have to find them a convent. You ruin them for the rest of us."

"To think I thought of you as friends," Warren mock-sniffed. "Turns out, all this time, Rachel was the only one."

John shook his head. "She was a soft touch. Couldn't be cruel to someone like you."

Warren smiled broadly. "I knew I was winning her over. Charming and irresistible, that's me."

"We need to finish cleaning up," I announced. "Because I need to get outside so I can puke."

"It's a good thing Rachel was cremated, or she'd be spinning in her grave," John added.

"I can see her now," I declared. "A dust devil whirling in her urn."

"Yeah, but she's whirling my way," Warren rebutted.

"You amaze me," John told him. "Never a success, yet you're positive you're what every woman needs."

"Of course I'm positive. Look at me. It's self-evident."

"Ah, the look of desperation," I quipped. "Willing to take advantage of the equally desperate."

"Whatever it takes, I suppose," John said. "But leave my sister out of your thoughts."

We all fell quiet. In my case, Rachel would always be the standard by which all others would be judged.

CHAPTER TWENTY-FIVE

Latisha, August 2000

Rose Ford would never get used to the slamming doors. She had no idea why Latisha needed to do it, why she was still there.

Over a two-year period, the slamming had gotten more frequent. It started with Latisha's bedroom. Then she moved down the hall and learned to slam one door after another as she passed. Then it was the bathroom door at the same time as her bedroom door.

Eventually, Latisha could close all the upstairs doors simultaneously. She'd shut them harder and harder until everything hanging on the walls rattled with every bang.

One morning, Rose walked into Latisha's room and found the alarm clock and all the pictures, books, and stuffed animals from the shelves and bookcases floating above the bed.

"Latisha," Rose stated. "I know it's you. And I expect you to put all of these things where they belong when you're done." A school picture of Latisha that normally sat on the headboard floated up to Rose and faced her. "You know I like you to keep your room clean. I'll make the bed." The picture floated away and joined the collection circling above the bed. After a few rotations, all the flying objects returned to their usual places.

A few days later, Rose went down to the kitchen to make breakfast for her and LaNaya. The cupboards were empty. All the dishes, pots, and pans spun in a five-foot circle two feet above the kitchen floor. As she watched, the circle became smaller but taller until a narrow column of spinning objects occupied the middle of the kitchen.

The silverware drawer slid open, and the contents joined the column at a faster pace as if the cutlery was racing and lapping the pots and pans. The things spinning the fastest seemed to move to the top of the column. Rose wondered if a tornado worked that way, too.

The door to the basement opened, and Mortimer ran up the stairs and through the kitchen. The cat stopped just inside the dining room, turned, and released a noise similar to what he had made the day the minister's plate of food had flown from his hand. It wasn't quite a growl, but it wasn't a meow. Certainly not friendly. More like a warning of an impending torrent of claws and teeth. Then he tore off through the living room and up the stairs.

From the dining room, LaNaya asked, "What's with Mortimer?" and walked into the kitchen. "Holy shit," she remarked. "Would you look at that?"

"LaNaya, don't swear," Rose admonished.

"I know, Ma, but look. It's like in the movies. My friends didn't believe me when I told them about doors slamming. They're never going to believe this."

"Latisha," Rose admonished. "Please stop."

"Ma, are you okay?" LaNaya asked. "Latisha's dead. She's not here."

The knives separated from the floating column. They zoomed across the room and stuck in the basement door. They were arranged in a nice, straight line from about head-high down to waist height.

"LaNaya, go pack some stuff and grab Mortimer," Rose urged. "We're going to visit Grandma Ford for a few days."

LaNaya nodded. "I like that idea. I can be ready in five minutes."

Rose spoke to the air. "Latisha, I'm sorry. I know you're angry. I'm angry, too, but this is too much. I can't stay here anymore. I don't know how to help." She turned and left the kitchen.

One by one, the kitchen items left the whirlwind and returned to where they belonged. "I'm sorry too, Mama. You're right. I'm mad as hell. And I know deep down, so are you." The knives pulled from the door in the opposite order they had stuck into it and returned to the butcher block stand, the magnetic strip above the stove, and the drawer they'd come from.

Latisha looked at the newspaper lying on the kitchen table. A pretty blonde graced the front page. "He's still out there. Someone has got to do something." She smiled. "I'd be happy to."

CHAPTER TWENTY-SIX

Daniels, September 2000

I managed to convince Mom to let me miss a day of school so I could attend the arraignment of the man who killed Rachel Thompson.

The courtroom was full. I somehow ended up with a seat on the center aisle about halfway back. Reporters from all the local television stations occupied the other side of the aisle. Recording devices must not have been allowed. No one had cameras or pocket recorders, only notebooks open on their laps. A few people in the front row held large tablets and sketched the defense and prosecution tables along with the people seated at them.

The lawyer for Rachel's killer was Ronald Logan, a thin man with silver hair in a charcoal gray suit. I'd seen his face on television but never listened to his commercials. I always hit a button and flipped to another channel before he could get started. He opened the proceedings by saying, "Your Honor, if it pleases the court, the defense asks that all charges be dropped for lack of evidence."

According to both the bailiff and the little sign on the bench, Judge McCall presided. The medium-sized woman with light brown hair looked over the top of her half-glasses at Logan and stated, "The Grand Jury felt there was sufficient evidence, and frankly, so do I. Besides, this is an arraignment, not a trial. Save it for then, counselor."

"The defense requests a change of venue."

"It's still too early for that, but denied."

"Your Honor, the defense…"

"Mr. Logan, it's too early for everything except reading the charges against your client. Please sit down and let us do that."

Next came a lot of formal court stuff I found boring but was probably necessary, at least from a legal perspective. It was unnecessary because I knew he was guilty. I heard charges of kidnapping and first-degree murder, along with a bunch of other things. At the end, Judge McCall asked, "How do you plead?"

Rachel's killer's voice was as gentle as I remembered. "Not guilty, your Honor."

I wanted to yell that he was lying or full of it or something, but I didn't want to get thrown out and miss anything.

Then Logan asked that his client be released on his own recognizance.

I thought the head of Harry Schmidt, the district attorney, was going to explode. He launched out of his chair. "Your Honor, the state asks that the accused be held without bail."

"And what is your justification for that, Mr. Schmidt?" McCall asked.

"He told us his name is Martin Franklin. We have found no documentation in any system to corroborate his claim." That was only the second time I heard the name of Rachel's killer. Even the news coverage did not include it. The name felt wrong to me. Maybe no one else had actually been able to confirm it.

Schmidt continued. "He does not have a permanent address. He appears to have no family, and we believe him to be a flight risk. The man is an enigma. Add to that a particularly heinous act against an innocent girl. We can't risk it happening to another while we wait for trial. He needs to be held without bail."

"Your Honor, my client has no criminal record, no history of violence against anyone," Logan insisted. "Besides being innocent, he's harmless."

I couldn't help it. I let out a snort. A few people, including the judge, looked my way.

"Where is your home, Mr. Franklin?" the judge asked.

"Wherever I happen to be, your Honor."

"Do you have a permanent address?" McCall asked.

"No, your Honor," Franklin claimed. "I'm between addresses."

"Until you're able to make arrangements for your client, Mr. Logan, and provide him with a permanent address, he will remain in custody," the judge pronounced. "If you come up with something, let the court know, and we will revisit the issue. Trial begins February second. Be ready, gentlemen. Court is adjourned."

CHAPTER TWENTY-SEVEN

Daniels, February 2001

I couldn't convince Mom to pull me out of school for the trial. She said it might take too long, and even I couldn't afford to miss that much school. She did drive me down so I could attend the first day, though.

The trial opened with Ronald Logan presenting a bunch of motions. He started again with asking for dismissal of all charges and requesting a change of venue. Then he moved that the arrest was made without probable cause, that the discovery of the body was done with an illegal search and should be tossed out, and that the judge should recuse herself due to bias against the defendant. By this time, Judge McCall was almost laughing at his requests. If anything, she was biased against the defense lawyer.

After that, Mom picked me up a few afternoons and drove me to the Hennepin County Courthouse so I could listen in on some of the proceedings.

The police had done an excellent job finding solid, scientific evidence to support the circumstantial stuff and what I knew to be true.

They reported finding the piece of rope in Franklin's pocket. It had skin cells from both him and Rachel on it, and it matched the marks around her throat.

The medical examiner, Dr. Andre Jordan, reported finding Martin Franklin's DNA in the form of semen in a few of Rachel's orifices.

A real estate agent testified that she'd called the police after finding one of her listings broken into. The responding officer had seen sufficient evidence to call in the crime lab. The crime lab found Martin Franklin's skin cells in the carpet of a house on the northwest corner of Queen Avenue North and Dowling Avenue. They also found Rachel's skin cells in the carpet, fibers on her that matched, and abrasions consistent with carpet burns on her back and side.

That would have been the house I stared at on my first day of searching. They may have been in it while I sat at the bus stop. Another sign that I'd failed Rachel. Some psychic.

Also at the house, the crime lab found a piece of finger-nail and a drop of blood that matched Rachel's. It was the nail from her little finger, and it was stuck in a door frame. In the nightmare with all the blood, the night before I found her, her little fingernail was broken.

A picture posted throughout most of the trial showed a close-up of Rachel with a large bruise on her cheek as if she had been punched.

I found one exchange between Dr. Jordan and the district attorney, Harry Schmidt, especially painful.

"Were you able to determine when Rachel died, Dr. Jordan?"

"Based on liver temperature and lividity, we approximated her time of death at between three and five a.m. on the day she was found."

I thought about my alarm clock after I woke from the nightmare.

There had to be a way to control whatever gift I had, to use it when it needed to be used. Not to have it tell me something happened that I should have prevented after it became too late.

If Officers Hanley and Morse testified, I missed it. I didn't see their names in the paper or on any of the news programs or websites. I also didn't see anything that said McLaren or Whitehead testified.

John told me none of the Thompsons had to testify, either.

Mom and I were both relieved that I didn't have to.

With the little evidence presented by the defense, it was surprising they didn't try to plea bargain their way out of it like they did on TV.

———

Mom pulled me out of school for the day of closing arguments. No revelations were presented, and Harry Schmidt came across as more convincing. The jury did not deliberate long. When court came back in session, Hanley and Morse sat in the back of the room. Mom and I sat with the Thompson family. When Martin Franklin was pronounced guilty, Mom and Mrs. Thompson began to cry. John gazed at the floor and sniffled. Mr. Thompson stared through the walls and into space.

I wanted to cheer, to jeer at Franklin and tell him, "I told you." I managed to restrain myself. Rachel probably would have wanted that, in spite of my knowing the truth from the moment I had first looked into his eyes.

Mom dropped me at the courthouse and went to hang with John and Mrs. Thompson while I attended the sentencing. Waiting two weeks to sentence Martin Franklin after finding him guilty made no sense to me. I'd arrived early, so I sat alone in the middle of the gallery, a few rows behind Mr. Thompson.

I was debating whether I should sit with him or not when Officer Hanley entered and sat beside me, his usual serious look frozen in place. Officer Morse sat on his other side. At least she smiled at me. "I know you're close to John and were with Rachel, but should you be missing school?" she whispered.

"I needed to see this through to the end. Let Rachel know we're still looking out for her."

The corners of Hanley's mouth moved as if he was smiling, and he nodded.

"Rachel knows," Morse claimed. "I'm sure she appreciates it."

"I still don't understand how you knew where to find her," Hanley mentioned.

"Neither do I."

"Tell us again how it happened. How it works."

I raised my brow. "Am I still a suspect, under interrogation?"

"No," Hanley declared.

"You were never a suspect," Morse added.

I looked at Hanley. His near-smile almost broadened. "Yeah, I checked you out."

"I knew it," I proclaimed. "I even told people you had."

Morse elbowed him. "You did? Why?" she asked. "And why didn't you tell me?"

"It was too convenient. Too strange how he knew. It would be easy to say he knew because he was the one who put her there," Hanley remarked. "I didn't tell you because you were convinced he was in the clear from the beginning."

"Instinct. It didn't feel right." Morse looked at me. "Besides, he doesn't look the type. Doesn't look big enough, either."

"No," Hanley agreed. "Rachel would have kicked his ass."

"You mean, beat me senseless and castrated me?" I asked.

They both laughed. People all over the courtroom, which was now almost full, including the people from the media, turned and looked at us.

"Yeah," Hanley muttered. "Something like that." To Morse, he explained, "He checked out okay and had alibis for the entire time leading to her estimated time of death, and for most of the time she was missing. Of course, one of the alibis was his mom. However, there was also John Thompson and both his parents, the staff at the Flying Dragon, the Coffee Nook, and Rocket's Car Repair. Not to mention a few cops who knew where he was." He looked at me. " I don't know about him not being the type, though. Something tells me if he had the justification, he'd be able to kill."

I could feel Morse's gaze on me. Out of the corner of my eye, I saw Hanley had gone back to looking straight ahead. I tried to look in the same direction. It was strange being the topic of conversation, especially when it revolved around being able to kill.

After a few seconds of silence, Hanley looked at me again. "So, how does it work?"

I should have asked, "How does what work?" but I didn't. Without looking at him, I admitted, "I have no idea. People ask me about something, and I just know. John says I have a variation of remote viewing."

"I've heard of that," Hanley replied. "Is it real?"

"The military uses remote viewing to locate targets. Psychics able to do remote viewing sit in a room and direct operations, tell whoever is out in the field where to find the bad guys," I told him. "Yeah, it's real."

"How is yours different?" he asked.

"Mine is more like remote following," I suggested. "I get a feeling and follow it where it leads."

"Is John psychic too?" Morse asked.

"No, but his mom is. I knew something was wrong, but she's the one who knew it involved Rachel."

"So, how does hers work?" Morse asked.

"She makes contact with something, sees a flash, and knows the reason for it. Sometimes, she blurts things out, completely unaware she said anything. John calls it tactile reception," I noted. "The day Rachel disappeared, she touched the doorknob and knew."

I went silent. They waited for me. I normally wouldn't feel compelled to fill the silence, but I continued. "By that time, my feelings had already told me something was wrong, so I knew Mrs. Thompson was right," I stated. "When it came time to find Rachel, I dreamed about her and knew things had turned bad. I mentioned to John that I had a dream about Rachel. Nothing specific, only a dream. He told me to find her. Somehow, I knew I could. I started walking, following feelings, until I ended up right in front of her."

I waited for more questions. When they didn't come, I mentioned, "What I haven't figured out is why Franklin was covering her body again. Why didn't he leave her and run?"

"You know, I wondered that, too," Hanley rejoined. "The only thing I can figure is he thought no one would believe you two, and he could hide her again and disappear."

"There is another option," Morse suggested. "He could have thought he was protecting her. That she belonged to him and would until somebody took her away."

"I guess that makes sense." I realized I was going to have to study psychology at some point. At least it didn't involve math. "You do realize that Rachel isn't his only victim, don't you?"

"Why do you say that?" Hanley asked.

"How do you know?" Morse inquired.

"Funny feeling. I just know."

Martin Franklin was brought in and seated at a table in front of the judge's bench. He looked around, took in the press and the spectators. His eyes stopped on Mr. Thompson, who suddenly turned and looked at him. Franklin smiled, one front tooth missing, then continued to stare around the gallery.

Mr. Thompson's hands moved to his sides and clenched. The tension seemed to radiate through his entire body until he was shaking. After a major tremor, probably when he realized he shouldn't go over the railing and try to kill Franklin, Mr. Thompson looked away, and the shaking subsided.

I was relieved John had stayed home. I wasn't sure he could have stopped himself the way his father had.

Martin Franklin's gaze met mine. We stared at each other. As the door to the judge's chamber opened, and the bailiff announced, "All rise," Franklin spoke to me.

"See you soon, kid."

I heard it perfectly clear in spite of the movement in the courtroom and the distance between us. And in spite of Franklin's lips never moving.

Then his lawyer touched his arm. Franklin looked away and got to his feet.

I sat and stared at the back of his head. I didn't look away until Hanley nudged me. I glanced at Hanley, saw the questioning look on his face, and went back to staring at Franklin.

Hanley leaned close. "Ready for what?" he whispered.

I looked at him. "What do you mean?"

"You said, 'I'll be ready.' Ready for what?"

"I don't know," I told him.

I didn't remember saying anything. I didn't remember hearing them announce Franklin's sentence. It didn't matter because I knew he wouldn't serve it.

Just another not-very-funny feeling.

CHAPTER TWENTY-EIGHT

February, 2001

Mrs. Thompson continued to lose weight. She kept moving as if busy work could block out the memories. In a short time, their house was so clean we were afraid to touch anything. Not that we were slobs or clumsy, but we didn't want to be responsible for more obsessive behavior. She was still quick to smile when she saw us, but the smile disappeared just as fast. As if her joy at seeing us had been driven away.

A few times, we found her standing in the doorway to Rachel's bedroom. As far as we could tell, she never went in anymore, only stared. John and I stayed out of Rachel's room as well. But we were more worried about upsetting his parents than disturbing any of Rachel's things.

Smiles never came to Mr. Thompson anymore. He seemed to have given up. He spent most of his time in the garage, sorting screws, searching for something he was sure he had and needed again. He no longer led the family on any excursions with me as the extra kid, didn't bother with most of the activities he used to enjoy. Warren and I helped John keep the sidewalks and driveway free of ice. One nice Sunday, we washed and vacuumed the cars.

Mr. and Mrs. Thompson started taking walks. As we watched them leave and return, it appeared they did not talk or get close enough that they might touch. Almost as if they were two strangers headed in the same direction at the same speed.

Then they started walking separately. I had to be sure they were okay, so I shadowed them a few times. Mrs. Thompson usually walked to the cemetery and sat at Rachel's grave. Mr. Thompson walked to Penn Avenue, then south to Rocket's garage, where he bought a candy bar and a soft drink, usually orange or strawberry. Then he would walk north until he got to the Daily Scoop on Forty-Fourth, where he bought an ice cream cone. From there, he circled west until he reached Victory Memorial Drive, then worked his way back home. At least I knew why he wasn't losing weight like his wife.

Neither of them went at a pace to suggest they were walking for fitness.

Without any discussion, John, Warren, and I started hanging out at my house. We also quit looking forward to tennis after the courts were clear. Without Rachel, we were missing our fourth. It shouldn't have stopped us, but it did.

We never talked about Rachel. I suspected the wound would always be too fresh, too deep for us to face.

We all acted like everything was fine, like nothing had changed. We were all lying and unwilling to face reality. So we went on. Maybe that was how people moved past tragedy. They fumbled along until something else happened to change their lives again.

CHAPTER TWENTY-NINE

<u>**April 2001**</u>

John found me at my locker. "Have you heard about the haunted house?"

"Do you mean the one on Fremont?" I asked. I was trying to decide if I wanted to take any books home with me.

"Yeah." He scowled. "You already knew? How? I just heard about it in English class."

"I've known for a couple of weeks," I declared. "What's a haunted house got to do with English?"

"We're in the science fiction and fantasy section."

"Okay, but why a haunted house?" I asked. "Or is horror included in your class? It isn't in mine."

"Why do you do this?" John asked.

I stared at him.

"We got talking about weird stuff," he explained. "That's all part of science fiction and fantasy. Then one of the kids asked Mr. Larson if he believed in any of that stuff."

"Which kid?" I asked.

"Thiessen. Does it matter?"

I nodded.

"Anyway, Mr. Larson said he didn't. He wanted more evidence," John remarked.

"And Thiessen asked him if he knew about the haunted house on Fremont?"

"Yeah. How did you know?"

"Thiessen is who asked me about it."

"Why?"

"He thinks I'm weird. He thinks I'm into that stuff."

"He's right," John stated.

I made a face like I had swallowed a bug or something. "How do you figure?"

"You're weird, and you're into that stuff."

"No. That's you."

"Quit denying it. It's you, too."

"Okay," I agreed. "So what?"

"So when are we going to check it out?"

Instead of looking at him, I stared at my English textbook. It was science fiction and fantasy. It didn't include any horror. Maybe they offered it at two different hours this semester simply to keep John and me apart. I had it right after lunch. Maybe they left the horror out to protect those with weak stomachs. "We're not," I stated. "It's an abandoned old house. Someday, it'll be condemned and torn down. It's not haunted. It isn't worth the trip."

"How do you know?" John asked.

"I don't."

John smiled and bounced on his toes. "Ha. You suspect something. Or you feel something. That's why you didn't tell me about it."

"What do you mean?" I watched him from the corner of my eye.

He couldn't stand still. "If you were sure, you'd have said you just know. I'd have believed you, and that would have been the end of it. Or you'd have told me it *was* something so you could see me all excited, then dash it to the rocks." He smiled broadly and bounced from one foot to the other. "Methinks you protest too loud," he quoted poorly.

I hadn't seen him this happy in a long time. I jammed the English book into my locker and swung the door shut. "Think so, huh?" I turned and walked away.

He nodded. "So when are we going?"

Sometimes John fixated on things, and this was sure to be one of them. The only way to resolve the issue was to go. Since the allegedly haunted house wasn't that far from school, and he appeared happy, we stopped by that afternoon.

The house was an old, almost-square, two-and-a-half story with a wrap-around porch. It sat toward the back corner of a double lot in a reasonably quiet part of the neighborhood. Most of the streets and sidewalks were gently cracked but passable and overshadowed by tall trees beginning to bud.

Behind the house, a one-car detached garage faced the alley. Somebody had scraped the siding, preparing it for a new coat of paint. The side window was boarded from the inside. All four panes of glass had broken. The top section of the garage door had fallen down. The service door lay in the knee-high grass. The garage damages made the lack of damage to the house more evident.

A chain-link fence surrounded the front and side yards, and a wood privacy fence circled the back. The way the house sat back from the road, combined with the fences and the double lot, made the place feel secluded.

It seemed strange that such a desirable property would be abandoned. Nothing suggested the people had moved out due to foreclosure, no signs posted for eviction or winterization. The place didn't look like it had been empty all that long. It certainly didn't look like the typical haunted house of my imagination. That would have been the big, rundown property across the street with the "For Sale" sign in the yard.

John and I stood on the sidewalk and watched. The front gate was open and hung a little crooked. Long grass from last summer drooped onto the concrete sidewalk. One of the four-foot squares was cracked and heaved up. An elm tree was trying to grow in the crack. The front steps had separated from the sagging porch. All things I'd seen in other houses I had looked at through the years with Mom. She said some settling occurred, though it wasn't anything that couldn't be fixed with a little time and a little care.

The two windows on the third-floor expansion were boarded from the inside, but the glass on both was still intact. Shades were drawn halfway on the first and second-floor windows. Again, none of the windows had been broken.

We stepped through the gate and moved up the side-walk. John stopped at the bottom step and looked at the door. I went as far as the top step and turned to face him.

His gaze slid from the front door to me. He swallowed hard. "After you."

I scowled at him. "How does this happen?"

"What?" His eyes widened, and the corners of his mouth turned up.

"You get me into something and make me lead."

"You're the leader," he claimed with a smile. "I'm the behind-the-scenes guy."

I didn't smile back. "You're the instigator. I'm the sacrificial lamb. I'm the guy on point. I'm the first casualty. I think that makes me the victim."

He shook his head. "Not a victim. A willing participant and almost never a casualty. You rarely bleed."

"Maybe a participant, but I don't know how willing."

"Okay, Daniels, what's the real problem?" John asked.

"Who says there's a problem?"

"If this was one of our normal adventures, you'd be busting through the door without any hesitation," he whispered. "You're obviously trying to convince me this isn't a good idea."

Since I was on the top step, I actually got to look down on him.

He gave me a knowing smile. "So, what's up?"

"Something doesn't feel right," I disclosed. "This isn't a good idea."

"Can you explain further?" His smile had turned smug.

"No. I only know we're not going to like what we find."

"You mean, like, we find nothing, and we're disappointed?" John asked.

I shook my head.

He smiled broadly. "You mean, like, the place really is haunted, and we find ghosts?"

I offered a combination cringe and shoulder-shrug.

"Well, I guess we have no choice," John decided. "After you."

I sighed, sagged, and looked at the ground. Then I watched as John started up the stairs. As I turned and took the last step onto the porch, I pointed at the uneven steps and the gap. "Let's remember this is here," I mentioned. "If we have to come running out the door, I wouldn't want you to break a leg trying to escape from some pissed-off ghost."

"Why do you think I'd do that?"

I stopped and looked at him.

"Oh, yeah. You're the graceful one. You're the first casualty, but I'm the one who gets hurt." He sighed and looked at the sky. "My family does seem to be the one to get damaged, doesn't it?"

I knew who he meant and chose not to say anything. "Even if we don't find anything, let's be careful. Okay?"

"Okay."

I made it to the welcome mat, then reached up and pressed the doorbell.

"Do you think that was necessary?" he asked.

"No, but it seems like the right thing to do."

"Unless it only alerts the ghosts to our presence."

"If there are ghosts, they already know we're here," I contended.

"Yeah, I guess." He nodded.

After waiting a few minutes, I pulled the screen door open and noticed a newer deadbolt compared to the old knob below it. A new lock should have told me we weren't getting in.

My hand went for the doorknob. The air was heavy.

"What if something finds us?" John asked.

I stopped, my hand hanging in mid-air.

"Right," he declared. "Let's be careful."

I nodded.

With my fingers suspended a few inches from the doorknob, I half-expected the door to open on its own. I realized that I hoped it would. When it didn't, I closed my eyes and grabbed the knob. I felt John looking over my shoulder as I gave it a turn.

The knob turned, the door opened, and for some reason, I wasn't surprised.

Why would an abandoned house be unlocked, especially considering the new deadbolt? Maybe whoever lived here had left in a hurry, or some homeless person had bolted after they stayed the night. Or maybe it was unlocked in anticipation of our arrival.

Yeah, right. I remained in psychic denial.

I pushed the door open and leaned in, staying on the balls of my feet. Silence greeted me. The air was heavy with dust, stale odors, and something else I couldn't describe. Neither could the gooseflesh on my arms.

John exhaled loudly, and my muscles tensed, prepared for the worst. The silence continued.

We stepped through the door, stood in the entryway, and tried to see as much as we could without actually venturing into the house. It was poorly lit, sunlight available only beneath the half-drawn shades. Since this was a spontaneous visit, we didn't have flashlights. After my eyes had adjusted, I moved further into the house. John was right behind me. We hadn't said a word, as if the spirits would only come to life and find us if we talked.

John pointed across the living room toward the kitchen. Even though he wanted to lead, I went first. I started toward the doorway, curious if we'd find the table set, the meal abandoned. I had read about something like that once and wondered what could make a family leave or disappear in the middle of a meal.

John stayed so close we were almost touching. Occasionally, he would lay a hand on one of my shoulders. I couldn't tell if he wanted to make sure I knew he was still behind me or if he was trying to steer.

I crept into the kitchen, then to the back door, and looked out into the yard. Another new deadbolt had been installed there. I wondered if it would have been locked if we had tried to use that door to get in.

A second door near the back exit looked like it would lead to the basement. A line of little slices, like the points of knives, had been pressed into the wood to create a pattern. My fingers wanted to touch, to see how deep they were, to learn why they were there. My abruptly climbing paranoia and the hair standing on the back of my neck suggested I didn't need to know.

I let my gaze cross the kitchen. The refrigerator was silent, its door closed. The oven was closed. Reddish-brown splatters adorned the stove top. Probably spaghetti sauce. Only a bouquet of dried flowers in a vase and an old newspaper occupied the aged, wooden kitchen table. The bottom half of the newspaper's front page was visible with a familiar picture in one corner.

I turned the paper so I could read it easier. The picture was Rachel Thompson, and the headline said she was missing. A dust-free spot remained on the table when I moved the newspaper. Everything else had a fine coating, undisturbed until we came. Yet somebody had been in the house as recently as last summer.

I looked over my shoulder at John. "Do we start in the basement or head upstairs?" My voice seemed to echo beyond the kitchen.

"I don't know," John rasped. "What do you think?"

I flashed him a give-me-a-break look.

"People die when they explore basements," he persisted.

I gave him a what-are-you-talking-about look.

"At least they do in the movies," he stated. When I shook my head, he added, "Yeah, I know, this isn't the movies." After a pause, he remarked, "Besides, you need to have sex to get killed by some monster."

I sighed and shook my head. "Since we don't have flashlights, it'll probably be easier to see upstairs. So let's start there."

John nodded. "Sounds reasonable. I like the way you're thinking."

I stared at him for a moment, then headed out of the kitchen. As we crossed the living room's hardwood floor, the only footprints visible were the ones we left.

I laid a hand on the carved wood railing and was about to climb to the second floor when John asked, "Did you see her?"

CHAPTER THIRTY

"See who?" I stopped and kept my gaze fixed on the riser to the third step.

"The girl," John stated.

I turned to face him. "Where?" I asked.

"Sitting on the couch." John stared at one end of the furniture in question. The old, overstuffed couch bore a pattern of mixed, swirling greens, maybe ivy or maple leaves.

I looked from John to the empty couch. "Where is she now?"

"Gone."

"Gone where?" I asked.

He shook his head. "I don't know."

No footprints appeared in the dust in front of the couch. No wrinkles in the cushions or the throw pillows. "Tell me what you saw."

We both stared at the couch, and he explained, "We were walking through the living room, and you were leading. Out of the corner of my eye, I saw a girl sitting on the couch, watching us. I turned to look at her, and she was gone."

"Describe her."

He closed his eyes and let his memory replay the scene. "Black girl, cute, about our age. Her hair was in little curls. I think they're called finger curls. She was wearing jeans and a baggy tee shirt from a blues festival."

"She was watching us?" I still stared at the couch.

"Yeah." John gazed at it, too.

"Did she think we wouldn't see her?"

"I think she wanted us to. Or at least me."

John was the only one who called me psychic. I seemed to know things. Gut feelings, mostly. If people asked, I said the feelings were funny, even though there was usually nothing funny about them. And I was able to find things. I simply knew where they were, where to look for them, or where they'd turn up. I didn't have visions, couldn't read minds, make predictions, or channel spirits. I never could make a Ouija board work.

Up until the moment he saw the girl on the couch, John had never displayed any psychic ability. His mom had a talent, but it didn't seem to pass on to him. He made up for lack of ability with endless curiosity that led him to absorb everything he could about extrasensory perception, whether it was plausible or not.

Great Grandma Nan may have visited on occasion, but I didn't believe it was her ghost. Only something creeping in or out of my subconscious. Sometimes in dreams, sometimes not.

John had seen girls in a cemetery that no one else could see. I don't believe he was delusional, then or now.

Of course, I could be wrong about pretty much everything.

However, neither of us had ever seen a ghost while hanging out in a supposedly haunted house.

I turned toward the stairs again. John reached out, touched my arm, and stopped me. We stared at the couch for a while longer. John and I alternated turning our backs to the couch, then looking from the corners of our eyes, a bizarre game of peekaboo. I walked to the couch and examined the cushions and dust. While I saw myself as a marvelous tracker, a perceptive and skilled hunter and explorer, my limited skills only stirred a dust cloud that made me sneeze, in turn liberating another cloud of dust from the cushion.

Nothing we did would bring the girl, ghost, or whatever back into our presence.

I shook my head and returned to leading our exploration. The stairs creaked as we stepped on them, but they didn't go flat and slide us to our deaths. The smooth wooden banister didn't come to life as a giant serpent and try to crush us. No one reached between the spires and grabbed either of us by the ankle.

Even though we hadn't said a word since talking about the girl sitting on the couch, I was sure John expected the same things to happen as I did. After all, we'd watched the same movies. Usually together and with Warren, and sometimes with Rachel. If Rachel joined us, she usually sat next to me so she could eat whatever snack I was working on. As a result, she'd use me as a shield. She would clench my arm or bury her face in my shoulder when something scared her. But it didn't happen often enough.

We took turns laughing at each other when one of us jumped at some scary part, like when the killer got up one more time. After watching the movies, we would tear them apart, discussing why they weren't scary or well-made or worth watching, even while the closing credits played.

I reached the top of the stairs and looked back. Not only could I not see the girl, I couldn't see the couch. I was at the wrong angle completely. Maybe on the way back down.

John and I exchanged a glance and shrugged. I turned and wandered down the hallway, which was about ten feet long with built-in drawers and cupboards in the walls. I peeked in one and found it full of towels. I poked my head into the four bedrooms and the bathroom. John waited at the top of the stairs, hand on the banister. He first looked down the hall, then down the stairs, then back to me. He was waiting for me to tell him to run.

In spite of not having been used for a while, the bathroom was neat and fairly bright. One bedroom was obviously for the parents. Another had things I thought belonged to a girl older than us, closer to Rachel's age. The third room contained a desk with a computer on it and a sewing machine.

I went to the fourth bedroom, furthest from where John waited. The one I thought belonged to the girl only John had seen, if this was actually her house. As I stepped into the room, John scurried down the hall and joined me. We stood inside the door and let our eyes wander. The room was bright and pleasant, decorated with pictures of kittens, flowers, and pop and hip-hop stars. The bed was made, and no clothes cluttered the floor.

When I exhaled, my breath came out in a little cloud. "Did you see that?" I asked.

"Yeah." John's breath didn't cloud. He waved his arm in front of me. "Cool! It's cold." He smiled. "It's a cold spot. A spirit just passed through here. A classic example of the paranormal. I've always hoped I'd experience one."

I gave him an are-you-crazy look. "So what does that tell us?"

"There's definitely something here."

"Where?"

"Here. In this house." He grew more excited, talking faster, beginning to bounce a bit. "We're not alone. This place is haunted."

"So?" I wasn't impressed or excited. At least, I wouldn't let him know I was.

"What do you mean, 'so'?"

"So, we've found a haunted house. What are we supposed to do with it?" I asked. "Give tours, charge admission, hope the spirits want to play?"

"I don't know," John admitted. "I've never had a haunted house before."

"That's just it. We don't *have* a haunted house. We don't know who it belongs to. We're trespassing. If the door hadn't been unlocked, we'd be guilty of breaking and entering. Are we supposed to catch your ghost? Transport it somewhere for study?"

John shook his head.

"Then charge admission so people can see our captive ghost? Even though she only showed herself once, and only to you."

His head-shaking grew more vigorous. "That's just..." He sighed. "You're crazy."

"Am I? I'll say it again. So we've got a haunted house. What are we supposed to do with it?" I inquired. "Tell the world?"

"I guess we're supposed to find out why it's haunted." He was suddenly very sure of himself. "Help the spirit pass on to..." he waved his arms broadly. "Wherever."

"Great. Besides being criminals, now we're supposed to be exorcists."

The closet door casually swung open like it was riding a gentle breeze.

Our feet stayed exactly where they were. We bent at the waist, stretched, and leaned, trying to see into the closet and behind the now-open door. When I looked back at John, his eyes were wide, and his mouth hung open. He swallowed hard. "I think this is where we're supposed to scream and run from the house."

"You're probably right," I agreed. "So let's not."

I drew a deep breath and stepped toward the closet. Clothes on hangers filled the clothes rod. A pair of faded blue jeans and a fuzzy yellow bathrobe hung on hooks attached to the wall. Another hook on the back of the door held a couple of belts, a pair of suspenders, and what looked like a cat collar. Three pairs of shoes lay on the floor to the right. To the left was a basket with a couple of sweaters and sweatshirts. Two small shelves above respectively held a couple of open shoe boxes with pictures sticking out and a small stack of books.

Though I should have expected something or someone

behind the hanging clothes, I delicately looked through them. Nothing helpful seemed hidden there.

I moved to the middle of the room and looked around. John remained glued to the same spot. At least he hadn't run yet.

A picture frame on top of the dresser had been turned toward the wall. As I watched, the frame slowly pivoted to face me. It contained a picture of a girl about our age with a Siamese cat. The girl was smiling. The cat looked as if it was trying to escape.

Some animals have trouble being cuddled. I'm one of them. Ask my mom.

"Did you do that?" John asked, his voice choked and dry.

"No." I shook my head and inhaled deeply. "I was hoping you did."

"I'm not telekinetic."

"I was afraid of that. Neither am I. That means we're still not alone."

"I told you," John rebuked.

I crept to the dresser and leaned forward to look at the picture. Then I blew off the dust. The picture didn't change, but I sneezed again. I gently lifted the frame from the dresser and examined it, then the picture itself. The girl's eyes drew me. I had the impression she was someone I could relate to, be friends with. Unfortunately, or maybe fortunately, I didn't recognize her. She lived within the boundaries that would have put her at our school, but I couldn't place her.

I tried to hand the picture to John. He wouldn't take it. After a few false attempts, he grabbed the edge of the frame with his fingertips and held it at arm's length while he looked at her.

"I don't know her," I remarked. "Do you?"

"Yeah," John stated. "She's the girl on the couch."

"I had a funny feeling you were going to say that. I meant do you know her from school?"

John pinched the picture with two fingers and handed it back to me. "No. I've never seen her before today."

"Great." I sighed. "She wants us here, doesn't she?"

He frowned. "What do you mean?"

"With the closet opening, the picture turning, her showing herself to us, or you. It's almost as if we're supposed to get to know her. To become interested or involved."

"Involved in what?" John asked.

"I don't know."

"Wherever this is taking us, I'm not sure I like it."

I closed my eyes, opened my other senses, and let my mind reach out. I smiled at him. "It'll be okay."

"A guess?" he asked.

"Funny feeling." The air somehow felt lighter, the sunlight sneaking past the shades brighter.

"That's good enough for me." He sounded relieved. "Should we go, or do you want to explore more?"

I slipped the picture into my backpack. John saw me and raised his eyebrows. "Since we're now thieves, too, I think we should leave," I told him. "Besides, we've got work to do."

CHAPTER THIRTY-ONE

<u>April 2001</u>

I told Mom another story about being in places that I shouldn't, doing things I shouldn't be doing. She seemed to accept it without question. Maybe she'd accepted my knowing things and using my feelings well and early enough in my life to consider it possible that I *had* been to a haunted house. Or maybe she believed in those things, too. Maybe she accepted what I told her because I was a teenager with a vivid imagination. Or maybe because I was her son.

It was possible she "just knew" things, too. Maybe someday I'd be comfortable enough to ask her. Instead, I asked, "Remember Officers Hanley and Morse? You met them the day we found Rachel."

"Of course," Mom replied. "Good, caring people. Professionals. I liked them. Why?"

"I need to talk to them."

"About your haunted house?" she asked.

I nodded. "If anyone can help me find out more, it would be those two."

She looked into my eyes. "Okay."

"After school, I'm going to take the bus to the Northside Precinct. I think they work out of there. I'm not taking John."

My mom looked a little puzzled.

"He's too nervous," I explained. "He'll freak, and I won't find anything out. I'll be okay going alone."

She gave me a smile. "I know."

After school, I hopped on the Metro Transit bus and rode to the downtown Minneapolis Police headquarters instead of the Northside Precinct house. Something told me I would find Hanley and Morse there instead.

I followed an officer through a side entrance into the building and walked down the hallways as if I knew where I was going. I smiled and acknowledged the people I encountered as I continued on my mission. A few officers watched me as I continued on. One police woman asked if she could help me. I told her no, that I was fine and knew where I needed to be. Acting like I belonged evidently meant I did to most people.

I made a series of turns, took a couple of flights of stairs downward, and found myself at the basement shooting range. I opened the door and peeked in to find Hanley and Morse, still in their uniforms, cleaning their weapons in an otherwise empty range.

"Just finishing a little practice?" I asked.

Morse jumped. Hanley actually reached for his gun, then asked, "Somebody leave the door unlocked?"

I smiled. "Actually, yes. And this wasn't the only one." I

looked around. "I would have expected better security, especially for a police station."

"I'll be sure to tell somebody," Hanley drawled.

"Then again, I suppose you don't expect anybody to actually break in, do you?" I asked. "I found doors unlocked someplace else, too."

Hanley regarded me through narrowed eyes.

"What brings you here, Daniels?" Morse asked. Her eyes were much softer, and she actually smiled.

"I needed to see you guys," I told her. "I need your help."

Her smile faded. "How did you know we'd be here?" she inquired.

"Funny feeling."

She shrugged. "Okay," she commented, then paused. "It's good to see you. Come, sit down and talk while we finish."

I perched on a nearby chair and watched as they worked in silence for a few minutes. I wasn't sure how to start. Fortunately, Hanley made it easy.

"What other doors have you found unlocked recently?" he asked.

I pulled the framed picture from my backpack and handed it to him. Morse tried to see it after Hanley gasped.

"What is it?" she asked.

"Latisha Ford," Hanley stated.

"Who?"

As if he hadn't even heard her question, he turned to me and gestured with the picture. "Where'd you get this?"

"I believe it was her bedroom."

"Do you know her?" Hanley asked.

I shook my head. "Not exactly."

His eyes locked on mine. "What were you doing in her bedroom?" he asked.

"We heard a story about a haunted house and decided to check it out. We saw a couple of things," I explained. "We ended up in what I believe was her bedroom, where I found the picture."

"When was this?"

"Two days ago."

"Who was with you?" he demanded.

There was no point leaving him out or lying to the people I needed to help me. "John Thompson."

"How is John?" Morse asked.

"He seems to be okay," I told her.

"Good. I was worried about him." Morse stepped closer to Hanley. "Richard, tell me what's going on."

He wiped his hand across the glass of the picture frame. He seemed drawn to her eyes the way I'd been. "Almost four years ago, Latisha Ford disappeared on her way home from school." He looked at me. "At the time, she was about your age now. She attended the same middle school. You would have still been in elementary school when this happened." He returned his gaze to her picture. "I was the one who found her. Everybody praised my thoroughness, but it was really blind, dumb luck." He almost smiled. "I couldn't let it go. Something about this girl's family…"

"And her eyes," I interrupted.

"Yeah." He paused. "Her eyes." He pointed at me with the picture. "I received a copy of this, too. Still have it. Something about her and her family just draws you in." He looked from Morse to me, then back to the picture. "Her mom told me I'd be the one to find Latisha's killer.

My luck didn't hold out. I still haven't found the bastard. The detectives let it get cold. It haunts me. Her older sister is quiet and reserved. Her mom is a wonderful woman, full of life. So was her dad. He died of a heart attack not long after. All this happening to one family isn't fair."

Hanley wiped the picture again. "Anyway, I was part of a group who looked for her after our shifts were over. Soft touches for missing people, I guess. Kind of like Rachel Thompson. The same group spent extra hours searching for her, too. With the addition of Linda." He smiled at Morse, then looked at me again. "You know the cemetery not too far from where you live?"

I nodded. "Where Rachel is buried."

"Yeah. I found Latisha there. Lying behind the tool shed in the far back corner."

"Oh my God," Morse stated. "This is the girl you were talking about the day we searched the cemetery for Rachel."

"It is," Hanley confirmed. "Latisha was covered with grass, leaves, and sticks. Like she was thrown into the compost pile. Pissed me off. You don't kill people and throw them away like that."

"Daniels, have you heard any of this story before?" Morse asked.

"Nope. Three years ago, I was working on my curve ball. I didn't listen to the news or pay any attention to girls. No matter what their story."

"When did you start searching haunted houses?" she asked.

"This was a new experience," I admitted. "I've always

loved spooky stories, cemeteries, whatever. I've never been to a haunted house, though."

"But you believe you have been now, don't you?" Morse asked.

"Yeah," I agreed.

"When you searched her house, did you see her?" she asked.

"John did."

"He recognized her?"

"When he saw the picture, he said that was who he saw sitting on the couch."

Hanley continued to stare at the picture. Morse laid her hand on his wrist. "I thought people haunted the place where they died," she remarked. "Was there any evidence she died at home?"

"Absolutely none," Hanley stated. "She was snatched walking home. Her mom called shortly after her sister arrived but Latisha hadn't shown. Rose Ford was a stay-at-home mom and made sure she was there when her girls arrived home from school every day."

"What happened to her family?" I questioned.

"I saw and heard a couple of unexplainable things when I was there after her father's funeral," he reported. "Plates flying, the cat screaming at nothing, doors slamming. I don't know if it continued afterward. I kept checking on them, and they seemed to be hanging in there okay. Then one day, they were just gone."

"Did they leave the door unlocked when they left?" I asked.

He shook his head. "No. Why?"

"Like I told you, it was unlocked when I got there. I

opened the door, and we went in. Like we were expected and welcome."

Morse shivered visibly. "Creepy. And hard to believe."

Hanley set the picture down, grabbed his weapon off the table, and holstered it. "Especially since I was there last week, and the place was secure. Both locks on both doors. I've been checking, keeping an eye on things. I feel like I should take care of them, still try to help."

They packed up their cleaning kits, extra cartridges, and guns in silence, then started for the door. I kind of hung out there, waiting. A few things about the conversation bothered me. When I could put a finger on them, I intended to ask more questions.

I followed Hanley and Morse to their car. They had finished their shift before they drove one of their squad cars to the downtown station for target practice. They'd parked out front in the middle of the street, a spot reserved for marked and unmarked police cars. They were loading their stuff in the trunk when Hanley smirked in my direction. "Were you hoping for a ride home?" he asked.

"No. I was hoping to finish the conversation."

"What's left?" Hanley asked.

"That's the problem. I don't know."

"Hop in," Morse invited. "We'll give you a ride, and maybe it will come to you."

We made our way to Seventh Street and took it north, away from downtown. Hanley drove, and I rode in the backseat. It wasn't a comfortable place to be. They were discussing dinner options when a few questions settled in my brain.

"Are you two more than co-workers?" I asked.

Their eyes met as they both turned to look at me. Morse almost smiled. "What makes you think that?"

"I don't know. Funny feeling."

Hanley returned to watching the streets, his scowl obvious in the rearview mirror.

"You two seem good together. I was just curious." I gazed out the window for a moment. "You said it looked as if Latisha had been thrown away."

Hanley met my gaze in the mirror and nodded.

"That was my reaction when I found Rachel," I told him. "That she'd been murdered and thrown away." I stared out the window again. "Was Latisha tied up?"

"There were indications that her hands had been bound and the ropes removed before she was put behind the tool shed," Hanley confirmed.

"Any other similarities between the two girls and their deaths that you can think of? Besides the way they were left, covered with whatever. Do we know where Rachel's killer was back then? What else haven't I considered?"

Morse turned to face me. "How old are you supposed to be?"

"Thirteen," I replied.

"Have you always been like this?" she asked.

"Like what?"

Her shoulders moved in an almost-shrug. "I don't know. Like you're older than you're supposed to be? Always having adult thoughts, talking serious? Like you think you're investigating something?"

I scowled. "I think so. It seems like a normal way to think and talk. The way I always have. Why? How am I supposed to be thinking or talking?"

"I don't know," Morse admitted. "I suppose you should be thinking about girls and using slang."

"I do my share of that, but some things are important." I almost snickered. "My mom wonders if I'm too serious sometimes. I remember her saying once that I was five going on thirty. Not to mention too curious."

"Make a deal with you," Morse stated. "Richard and I will look into things further if you'll go back to being a kid."

It seemed like a reasonable idea. "I guess that'll be okay." I tried to imagine how I would feel sitting in the back of a police car if I had actually done something. "You never answered my question earlier."

"Which question?" Morse inquired.

"About you two."

Hanley adjusted the mirror so I couldn't see his eyes. Morse turned back to the front. "We're friends, too," she told me.

We rode in silence the rest of the way to my house. After we pulled up to the curb in front, Hanley put the car in park and turned to face me. "Something you said earlier has been bothering me, and I want to make this perfectly clear while the three of us are together. You asked, 'What else haven't I considered?'"

I nodded in confirmation.

"You're not supposed to be considering anything. You're supposed to be in school and staying out of trouble. You should still be working on that curve ball. And staying out of an official police investigation."

"My curve ball is good for nothing but beaning people. Same with my fastball. No matter how careful I aim, my pitches seem to go straight at the batter. It's pointless. Ask John and Warren. They used to be my primary targets. Now, if we play, they won't let me pitch," I remarked. "And two dead girls invited me into this investigation, so I might as well try to help."

Hanley opened his mouth, but Morse stopped him by laying her hand on his arm. "You are, and you have," she declared. "Let us take it from here, though. If we think of anything else, we'll come and talk to you."

I looked from one to the other and back again. It didn't seem like a good idea. I went along with them anyway. "Fair enough. As long as I don't receive any more messages from dead girls."

Hanley tried to smile. Maybe it was as successful as he got when he smiled at anybody other than Morse. "I guess we'll have to resolve this quick so you can hang around with live ones instead."

I glowered at him as Morse got out of the car to open my door. There was no handle on the inside, no escape permitted. "I'm not sure I'm ready for girls of any kind at this point. Way too complicated."

Morse laughed. "We women are not complicated until we let men into our lives. Then, all hell breaks loose."

She climbed back into the car. They both waved as they drove off.

CHAPTER THIRTY-TWO

May 2001

"I'll catch up to you later," John told us and left me and Warren standing by our lockers. Warren was staying after for some activity he wouldn't disclose, so I decided to follow John.

I hadn't seen where he went. By the time I got outside the school building, he was nowhere to be seen. I stood at the edge of the sidewalk, faced away from the school and into the sun, and closed my eyes. And I knew where to find John.

Even though Rachel wasn't there, only her ashes, I had stopped by the cemetery one day. I sat on her grave and remembered the time we'd spent together. Playing tennis, hanging with her family, helping her recover from her broken leg. I laughed again at some of her insults. Like the one she'd landed the day we finally met. She walked in, looked at John and me, and announced, "Who's the little creep?" When John replied, "That's Daniels," she told him, "I wasn't asking you. I was asking him."

Like that one, most of her insults were directed at John. Although she'd lobbed some good ones in my direction, too.

I don't consider myself a down person. Not prone to bouts of depression. A bit angry at times, but I'd felt better after spending the time thinking about her.

I looked across the cemetery, between the rows, and spotted John. I could understand why he made trips to her grave. I didn't understand why he thought he shouldn't tell us.

As I approached, John stopped reading out loud and looked up at me. He was sitting on the ground, his back to somebody else's stone.

"What are you doing here?" he asked.

"I came to keep you company."

"Why?"

"Because I miss her, too," I replied. "What are you reading to her?"

"*Audrey Rose* by Frank DeFelitta." John held up his book.

"A bit old, but a fun read," I remarked. It was about some people trying to save their daughter, who was the reincarnation of someone who died badly. "Didn't I give that to you?"

"You did," John confirmed. "I'm finally getting around to reading it." He closed the book and set it on the ground.

I sat next to him. "Do we know whose stone we're leaning on?"

"Someone named Anderson. There's a ton of them around here, so I don't think it's anybody we know."

"As long as they don't decide we're being disrespectful. I don't know about you, but whenever I walk through these places, I think I'm supposed to stay off the graves and try to find aisles. Just seems right."

"Then there's the old 'if you stay off their graves, they can't grab you,'" John added.

"Yeah, that's true," I agreed. "But that's not what I think about when I stay on the sidewalks and aisles."

John craned his neck. "What the…"

I followed his gaze directly ahead past Rachel's stone. "What is it?"

"Did you see anyone else in the cemetery when you came in?" John asked.

"No. I think we have the place to ourselves. And the dead, of course."

"This is not the time to think you're funny," he stated.

"Warren is the one who thinks he's funny. I'm only your run-of-the-mill smartass."

"It's still a cry for attention," John expressed. "Look. There they are again."

"Who?"

"Three girls. I think they're playing tag."

"Girls? Playing in a cemetery?"

"Exactly," John rejoined. "A while ago, it might have been us. Now, that would be too weird. We couldn't do it."

"I don't see them," I remarked.

"How can you not? They're coming this way."

"How many?" I asked.

"Still three."

"Have you seen them before?"

"Yeah, actually. I have," John confirmed. "They were three of the girls in the cemetery the day of Rachel's funeral."

"I didn't see them then, either," I told him.

"You believe me, don't you?"

"Why wouldn't I?" I professed. "We keep sharing all these strange events. It's too late to start questioning anybody's sanity but my own."

"You really don't see them?"

"No."

"You don't see them standing right in front of us, looking right at us?"

"This must be your ability because, no, I can't see anybody." My legs were extended out in front of me. Something pushed my left foot, so it rocked to the side and back up. "What was that?" I questioned.

"That's how close they are," John explained. "One of them pushed your foot with hers."

"Do you have hair growing in new places?" I asked.

"What?"

"I spend too much time with you to know if your voice is changing, so I was wondering if you're going through puberty," I replied.

"How can you worry about that now?"

"All of the stuff we've read suggests that, for some people, the release of psychic abilities is triggered by puberty," I told him. "You've always wanted to believe that everybody has a psychic ability but some aren't able to access it. Maybe you're right. Maybe your ability is to see ghosts, and it's arrived with these three and Latisha Ford."

The other option in our reading was that some type of stress released psychic abilities. I didn't want to suggest that his sister being murdered may have triggered him.

Then I wondered if the release of psychic ability was what turned some people into psychopaths.

"I've got hair where I should," he declared.

"Good. Glad to hear it," I told him. "And now you can see dead people."

"But not all the time." He drew a fast inhalation. "Oh, God, I think I'm going to be sick."

"What's happening?" I asked. "Quick, tell me about it. Describe them."

"The one closest to you is a few years younger than us. She's wearing a light jacket. It's pink and white. Except for the blood stain next to the torn shoulder."

"Memorize her face," I suggested.

"Already have it. You know my memory," he told me. "Except now her cheek is melting. It's sliding down her face. Yep, I may have to puke."

"Only remember her face before her cheek melted," I instructed. "Memorize her face when it's whole."

"I'll try, but as good as my memory is, I may not be able to shut things out." John closed his eyes, then slightly turned his head and opened them. "The girl standing in front of me is about our age. She's wearing a Girl Scout uniform. She's earned a lot of badges. She's holding a box of cookies. They're Thin Mints."

"Try to memorize her face, too," I urged.

"You know I can do that. You don't even have to tell... Ah, jeez. I really am going to be sick."

"What is it?"

"Her uniform, right where her...legs come together," John blurted. "All of a sudden, there's a blood stain, and it keeps growing. Oh my God, I can't do this."

"You'll be okay," I urged. "We need to do this. They're not here to hurt us."

"How do you know?"

"Funny feeling. I just know," I stated. "Because they already would have. After all, we're sitting here like a couple of dummies waiting to be slaughtered."

"I suppose you're right."

"Of course I am," I remarked. "Tell me about the third one."

"She's tall, must be about Rachel's age. She might be as pretty as Rachel."

"That's tough because I think Rachel was beyond pretty."

"Well, you'd be saying that about this one," John pointed out. "She might have bigger, um, you know, than Rachel, but wow." He rubbed his hand across his face. "Can I memorize more than her face?"

"Of course," I agreed. "Tell me more."

"She's wearing jeans and a tee shirt. Oh, shit, not her, too." John blanched. "Her shirt just tore away. Her bra pulled down, and her breast...it's turning. It's like it's being twisted and pulled, and somebody hurt all three of these girls and *I can't take it.*"

He jumped to his feet and ran. I didn't know what to make of the girls since I hadn't seen them, so I grabbed his book and took off after him.

John made it about three rows before he stopped against a large stone. He bent over it and woofed his cookies all over somebody's grave.

I stood beside him, looking back toward Rachel's headstone.

He groaned. "It's not fair. I finally have an ability, and I'm not sure I want it." He spat on the ground, then wiped his face with the back of his hand, which he then wiped on his jeans. "Is this how you and Mom feel?"

"I don't think we have a choice in any of this," I suggested. "Things come to us, and we're supposed to deal with them."

"How are we to do that?" he asked. "What have we done about the girl in the haunted house?"

"Well, actually, I've got Hanley and Morse working on that one," I informed him.

"We broke into a house, stole a framed picture, and you went to the police?"

"We didn't break in," I countered. "Somebody let us in."

"How do you figure?"

"The house was locked the week before when Hanley stopped and checked on it," I declared. "He's the one who found that girl."

"The one in the picture? He found her?" John asked. "Is she okay?"

"No. He didn't find her until after she was dead. He's the one who found her body."

"Did he find her killer?" John inquired.

"No. They took him off the investigation, gave it to the detectives."

"That was dumb."

"I agree. Morse and Hanley are who I'd want working on it. The three ghosts you saw today, who were at Rachel's funeral, none of them are Latisha Ford, right?"

"That's right," John confirmed. "Does that matter?"

"Hanley found Latisha Ford's body in this cemetery. She wasn't alone here."

His fists went to his temples. "I don't want to think about it." He looked back toward Rachel's grave. "I have to go get my book. I'm not sure I want to."

"It's okay. I brought it with me." I handed it to him. "How many times have you been to Rachel's grave?"

"I think six," he guessed.

"And you've never seen the girls any of those times?"

"No. Only the day of Rachel's funeral, when there were more than three. And today, after you came, when they were all standing around the grave."

"That seems odd," I remarked. "Why can't you see them when you're alone? Aren't they there then, too?"

"I'd think so," John declared. "But the more I learn about this psychic shit, the less I know."

"Kind of like math," I offered. I turned and walked toward the entrance to the cemetery. John followed until we got to a concrete path, then stepped up beside me.

"I think we need to call Hanley and Morse. See where they are on the girl in the picture and tell them about the girls today," I suggested, then turned and looked back again. "There has to be something we can do. Something we're supposed to do."

CHAPTER THIRTY-THREE

During our previous encounters, Morse and Hanley had both given me their business cards. Figuring Morse was the friendlier of the two, I called her first. She answered on the third ring. "Linda Morse."

"This is Jacob Daniels."

"How are you, Daniels?"

"Not really sure," I admitted. "Something has come up, and I think we should talk."

"Okay," Morse agreed. "Let's talk."

"Not on the phone. We need to meet."

"If you think that's best. When?"

"As soon as possible."

"Can you tell me what this is regarding?"

I frowned. "Not really. I'm not comfortable discussing it over the phone."

"Okay."

"Besides, Officer Hanley and John Thompson need to be in on the conversation from the beginning."

"Okay. When can you and John meet?"

"Any time," I told her. "We're together now."

"Should we come to one of your houses?"

"No, that probably isn't the best idea. How about we meet at the Daily Scoop on Forty-Fourth?"

"Ah, ice cream," Morse enthused. "Good choice. Give us an hour, okay?"

"Perfect. See you then."

After making sure Mr. Thompson wouldn't be going for a walk, John and I rode our bikes to the Daily Scoop. I waited outside while John went in. He emerged with a giant double scoop of peanut butter swirl in a waffle cup with caramel drizzled over the top.

"I thought you always went for the flavor of the day," I remarked.

"I did, but your lack of enthusiasm made me reconsider. And I agreed. Raspberry cookie crumble was not the best choice for meeting the police."

Morse and Hanley pulled into the small parking lot in a police cruiser. They got out of the car and walked up to us. Hanley stared while Morse smiled and turned to the sign in the window. "Raspberry cookie crumble. One of their best flavors," she proclaimed.

Hanley nodded, then looked at my lack of ice cream and John's monster waffle cup. "You go ahead. I think I'd better pass." He used a muscular arm and a giant hand to pat his flat stomach. "I had too much lunch today, anyhow."

"Suit yourself. My lunch didn't cut it," Morse claimed. "Don't expect me to share." She went in to place her order.

Hanley looked at John's ice cream again. "I think I'm getting a sympathetic sugar buzz just watching you." He pointed. "It's starting to drip down the side."

John turned the waffle cup, glanced at the ice cream trail, and began licking furiously. When Morse came back out, the side of John's cup was drip-free, and he was dabbing at his lips with a napkin.

Morse bit her ice cream, then held it toward Hanley. "This is really good. Too bad you're not going to have any."

"Yep," Hanley drawled. "Too bad."

The four of us approached the cruiser. Hanley sat on the trunk, and the rest of us kind of circled around him. "So, what did you want to talk about?" Hanley asked.

"For one, I was hoping for an update on Latisha Ford," I told him.

"Well, as I told you, I found her body. Detectives McLaren and Whitehead led the investigation."

"They were lead when Rachel went missing, weren't they?" John asked.

"Yeah, they were," Morse confirmed.

"I wasn't too impressed," I stated.

"Really?" Hanley asked. "Why not?"

"I didn't think they took our initial concerns seriously enough. After they decided she might actually be missing, it felt like they still wanted to believe she had run away, and they weren't going to look too hard to find her."

"They're good cops. Been doing it a long time," Hanley commented. "I should probably be pissed for letting you talk about them that way."

"But?"

"But you may be right," he conceded. "I remember thinking Latisha's case went cold too quickly, and at one point, I wondered what they'd been doing."

"I suspect you've been stirring things up a bit since we last talked," I suggested.

"And why would you think he'd be doing that?" Morse asked with a smile.

"McLaren and Whitehead relied too heavily on the usual profile," Hanley explained. "Latisha's hands had been tied, and there had been a rope around her neck at some point. Hers was the only body we had, so we didn't know what to compare her murder against."

"Then I found Rachel," I filled in.

"Yeah, but while her hands had been tied and there had been a rope around her neck, she was a different age and race."

"She didn't fit the profile," I remarked. "Which was created using too small of a sample."

"Right," Hanley agreed.

"So no one compared any DNA or patterns of behavior that might put them in similar situations?"

"Not until you came to us with Latisha's picture," Hanley divulged. "They're running the DNA now and are going back through everything in the file."

"How do you know so much about this stuff?" Morse asked.

"I've been reading Thomas Harris and Patricia Cornwell," I stated.

"Those are fiction, aren't they?" Morse asked.

"Yes, but good fiction is always anchored in some kind of truth."

"You're a little young to be reading things like that, aren't you?" she inquired.

"Probably."

"Doesn't it give you nightmares?"

"I have nightmares already. Almost every night," I revealed. "Nightmares triggered by or mimicking things I've read and seen usually aren't as scary as the ones that come out of nowhere."

"Really?" Morse asked. "Should you be talking to a professional?"

"Probably," John and I chorused.

"Except he'd probably scare them into early retirement," John added.

"I'm becoming convinced the nightmares are linked to my ability to find things," I stated.

"You'll remember I was actually the first to suggest that link," John put in.

"You did. Doesn't mean I can't become convinced, does it?"

"No, of course not," John offered. "It's like your first step to admitting you're a psychic."

"That's probably not a good thing, is it?"

Hanley snorted. "No. Because then you'll never stop."

"Stop what?" I asked.

"Getting involved where you shouldn't," he clarified. "Which is why we're here, isn't it?"

"John saw something that got me thinking," I admitted.

"Oh, shit," John declared.

"I agree," Hanley chimed in.

"I think we need to compare days when girls went missing in this part of the city with days they held funerals in the cemetery where Rachel is buried. Where you found Latisha Ford," I suggested.

"That might be tough," Morse advised. "I don't know if

we can get all that information and pull it together. What are we trying to find?"

"We also need to sit John down with a stack of pictures of missing girls. Or maybe a sketch artist," I declared without answering the question.

"What are you up to, Daniels?" Hanley pressed.

"And we need to disregard certain aspects of the profile and simply compare how girls have been getting killed."

"Daniels, stop. Answer our questions," Morse ordered.

"I'd love to, but I'm trying to get all mine out before they disappear."

"If you tell us why, we may be able to ask some more pertinent questions," Hanley encouraged.

"You don't have to do this alone," Morse remarked.

"This is why I'd prefer you never admit to being a psychic," Hanley pointed out. "I don't want to believe in psychics. Or that you are one. Or that you're never going to quit getting involved."

"John, you know where I'm going with this," I noted. "You'd better start at the beginning."

"The day of Rachel's funeral, I saw some girls wandering around the cemetery," John explained. "It almost looked like they were playing hide and seek."

"How far from where we were?" Morse asked.

"A couple of them were kind of close. A few stayed quite a ways away."

"How many were there?" Hanley asked.

"I'm not sure," John replied. "At least six."

"At what point in the service did you see them?" Morse questioned.

"At different times throughout the service. They'd

appear and disappear, then reappear somewhere else. That's why I thought they might be playing hide and seek or tag."

"Who would play hide and seek in a cemetery?" Morse wondered.

"Well," I admitted. "Once upon a time, we might have been weird enough to think it would be fun and scary."

"During an actual funeral?" Morse asked.

"Probably not then," I decided. "That would have been pushing it, even for us."

John nodded. "I agree. No matter how weird we are, we'd still be respectful."

"We might attend the funeral, but we'd be respectful," I stated.

"Great. Remind me not to have sons," Morse quipped.

"You won't," I told her. "You'll have daughters."

"Really?" she asked.

"Yeah."

"Wait. How could you possibly know that?" Morse blurted. "Or even pretend to know? How could you even say such a thing? It isn't something you should be joking about."

"I'm serious about you and daughters. I just know it," I responded. "Funny feeling."

"I'm growing to hate those things," Morse grumbled.

"Already do," Hanley confirmed.

"Me, too. The problem is Warren and I did not see the girls in the cemetery."

"I don't remember seeing anybody outside the funeral in the cemetery, either," Hanley professed. "Not even workers."

"So, we're at the cemetery today, and John tells me he sees three girls among the markers," I revealed.

"They were three of the ones I saw during the funeral," John expounded.

"Which means either ghosts are gathering in the cemetery, hanging out and finding people to visit, or there are other girls buried where they shouldn't be. Waiting to be found," I proposed.

"You want John to look at pictures of missing girls to see if he can find any of the ones you saw today," Morse suggested.

"Right."

"You're thinking girls went missing a few days before a funeral, then were murdered and left in the cemetery?" Hanley asked.

"The theory I'm working on now is that they're buried there," I remarked.

"Wouldn't the people who dug the graves have seen somebody hanging around?" Morse questioned. "Or seen a body when they filled it in or made sure it was ready for the funeral?"

"Who checks a grave to make sure it's empty before they place a body in it?" I asked.

John's brow went up. "Nobody. It's assumed nobody wants to be in one, so why would they go there?"

I continued my theory. "It would depend on when the grave was dug. If it was the day before, someone could sneak in at night, dig a bit deeper, put a body in, and fill the grave to where it had originally been. Then the casket goes on top. And someone comes along later, fills the grave, and finishes burying both bodies."

"Interesting," Hanley mused. "What if the grave was dug the morning of the funeral?"

"In that case, the killer is probably part of the digging crew," I suggested.

"Which means you need to check employment records, too," John pointed out.

"That might be tough," Hanley contended. "Sometimes the cemeteries use day labor and temporaries for the landscaping and digging. Especially if they're not using a backhoe."

"They may not keep the best records if they paid in cash," Morse added. "Could make it tough to match anything."

"And I don't think too many cemeteries would be worried about hiring sex offenders to dig graves," Hanley further mused. "It's plausible."

"But we can't go around digging up the cemetery," Morse advised. "We don't have enough proof."

"Can you get underground radar?" I asked.

"Ground-penetrating radar?" Hanley considered that. "They've used it for measuring the depth of glaciers, but I don't know what else they've done with it. Would it work here?"

"It might," John posited. "Unless the metal caskets block it."

"I know the Minneapolis Police doesn't have anything like that," Hanley stated.

"That's why we have to start by matching funeral days to missing girls," I revealed. "Narrow down the area we have to check, so when we get a method that works, we don't waste it."

Morse nodded. "Let's start with the pictures. What do your parents think you're doing right now?"

"Having ice cream," John announced. His cone had developed a leak, so he was again licking furiously.

"Why don't we come over tomorrow afternoon when you're home from school?" Morse offered. "We'll bring some pictures for you to look at."

"That'll be fine," John agreed.

"Let's do it at my house," I urged.

"Yeah, that probably would be best," John declared. "My parents aren't the same. I don't think they're handling all this too well. It might not be good to bring the police back into the house."

"Do you think they should be handling it differently?" Morse asked.

"Probably not," John conceded. "It's just tough to watch."

"I'm sure it is," Hanley remarked. "I can't even imagine how they're feeling."

I grunted. "Neither can I, nor do I know. Further evidence I'm not psychic."

CHAPTER THIRTY-FOUR

Hanley and Morse arrived at our house wearing street clothes, carrying file folders and a six-pack of Mountain Dew. "You guys drink this stuff, right?" Hanley asked.

"Or something very similar," John agreed.

"Pretty much non-stop," I added.

"Me, too." Hanley started pulling cans from the plastic rings. "Linda has more willpower." He handed her one.

"This will be my only one today," she announced.

"How do you live?" I asked.

"Coffee. Strong and black."

"Sounds like my mom," I replied.

"Speaking of your mom, did she know we were coming over?" Morse inquired.

"I told her. She knows about the haunted house and that I came to you for help. I said you had some follow-up questions and some pictures you wanted us to see."

"Not far from the truth," Hanley remarked.

I led them into the kitchen. We each took a chair at the table. "So, what have you got?" I asked.

Hanley opened his folder and laid pictures out on the table. "See if you recognize any of these people," he requested. When he stopped, sixteen pictures were spread before us.

John reached out, his fingers hanging in the air, slowly waving above the pictures as they mirrored the movement of his eyes. "Are all these girls missing?"

"No," I told him. I reached past his hand and lifted a picture. "She's a cop." I handed the picture to Hanley, who slid it into the file folder without saying a word. I lifted another picture and gave it to Morse. "She's somebody you know. You went to school with her or something."

"What makes you say that?" she inquired.

"Funny feeling," I remarked. "Thought you'd throw in a couple of ringers, see if you could catch us."

"Standard procedure in any lineup," Hanley claimed. "I thought you just found things."

"That's one of his tricks," John revealed. "He also just knows things. But he says he's not psychic." His fingers stopped, then descended to the table. He lifted a picture of a girl with freckles, brown hair, and blue eyes. "She was in the cemetery. Came and stood right in front of us," he announced. "She's a Girl Scout, and she's dead."

"You're positive?" Hanley asked.

"My memory is excellent. Almost eidetic," John pointed out. "Yes, I'm quite sure."

"How do you know words like that?" Hanley challenged.

"I read the dictionary. After that, I can't forget them."

"She's missing," Morse confirmed. "Almost six years now."

"You've never found her body?" I asked.

"No," Hanley declared.

"Or her killer?"

"No."

John lifted another picture. "She's one of the girls who was playing hide and seek the day of Rachel's funeral. She didn't come up to us with the others." The girl was blonde with curly hair. Her makeup made me think she was in a dance performance or something. "She's dead, too." He sniffled, stood, and walked over to the sink. He made a production of washing his hands. I thought it was a little odd until I saw him use the towel to wipe his eyes, too.

"You okay?" Morse asked as he returned to the table. "We don't need to do this."

"Yes, we do," John insisted. "I'll be okay." He pulled his arms across his chest, almost as if he were giving himself a hug. "Your sample of pictures is too small," he proclaimed. "These are mostly white, with one Asian and one black girl. It isn't the right black girl, there were no Asians, and there was at least one Native American in the cemetery."

Morse opened the file folder she was holding and laid out another half-dozen pictures. John immediately lifted one of a black girl. It was probably her school picture or from another event, maybe even a Glamour Shots photo. He handed it to me.

"Wow," I commented.

"I told you about her," John advised.

"You did?"

"She's the one who was about Rachel's age and might have been as pretty."

"Oh yeah. Well, you weren't lying," I agreed. "She was

definitely competition for your sister." I handed the picture to Hanley, who looked at it but didn't say anything.

John lifted two more pictures. "These two were in the cemetery." One was a Native American girl about our age, the other a white girl a few years younger.

"We have a problem," Morse announced. "The girls in those last pictures weren't from this end of town."

"Snatched somewhere else and brought here?" I wondered.

"Maybe. We won't know until we find their bodies."

Hanley held out the picture of the black girl. "She was competition for Rachel. She was already doing some modeling, a few fashion things for places like Target."

"Definitely wow," I stated.

"She was last seen in South Minneapolis when she left an advertising agency after a photo shoot," Hanley revealed. "That was fifteen years ago."

Morse tapped the picture of the Native American girl. "She was taken just off East Franklin Avenue in southeast Minneapolis, not far from the river. She had left a friend's house and was walking home. She was supposed to be there in time for supper, but she never made it. The friend only lived three houses away, so she may have been taken from right in front of her own house. That happened about nine years ago."

"How old is Martin Franklin?" I asked. "When did he start?"

"Why do you think Martin Franklin killed all these girls?" Hanley wondered.

"Funny feeling. If you remember, I once told you that Rachel wasn't his only victim."

"I remember," Hanley declared.

"Well, we've found some more."

Nobody said anything as Morse gathered the pictures and returned them to the two file folders.

"You brought the second folder of cold cases from other neighborhoods, not really believing they'd be included in what John saw," I remarked.

"Honestly, we thought this whole thing was a stretch," Morse admitted.

"You really saw these girls?" Hanley inquired.

"Yeah." John looked at me. "And you really didn't?"

"No. I've never seen any of them before."

"This is just too weird," Morse stated. "I don't know how we can convince anybody to dig up the cemetery."

"Martin Franklin has been killing girls from all over the Twin Cities for at least fifteen years. You've only found a couple of bodies, and there's never been enough evidence to even look at this guy?" I asked.

"He's not in the system," Morse professed.

"And we've never seen him around," Hanley added. "He never came up in an investigation. He's never mentioned anywhere. Not until you found him."

"Maybe this so-called gift, which to me isn't one, is good for something after all," I claimed. "Remember when we wondered why he was still around Rachel so we could catch him?"

"Yeah, I remember that," Hanley agreed.

"He came back to move her," I remarked.

"And Latisha Ford was supposed to wait in the compost pile until he could get back and put her into a grave some-where," Hanley postulated.

"So we're lucky we found the two bodies we did?" Morse suggested.

Hanley nodded. "Looks like it."

"So what's next?" John put forth. "Am I supposed to hang out in the cemetery and see if these girls will tell me something?"

"That's one idea," I answered.

"Why couldn't you have been the one to see them? You're much better at talking to girls than I am."

"And I'm not very good at it, either. It's too bad this isn't Warren's gift."

"Yeah. After all, he thinks he's a gift."

"I think we really need to compare burial dates with the missing girls," I declared. "Maybe, if things match, somebody would let us dig one up so we can check beneath their coffin."

"I'm beginning to think underground radar might be the answer," Hanley stated. "If it will work in a cemetery."

"What about methane sniffers?" John wondered.

"You guys have been spending too much time on this kind of stuff," Morse professed.

"If we're looking at fifteen-year-old murders and burials, I don't think there will be anything left decaying," Hanley estimated. "It may be too late for methane sniffers."

"Wouldn't all of the dead people in the cemetery mess up a methane sniffer, anyhow?" I challenged.

"I suppose they would," Hanley agreed.

"I'm going to be cremated," Morse insisted. "But not for a long while."

"Really long," I remarked. "After all, you need to have your daughters."

CHAPTER THIRTY-FIVE

I found a new way home from school and used it almost every day that I walked alone. As John didn't want me to know he was going to the cemetery, I didn't want him to know I was going to Latisha Ford's home on a regular basis.

Some days, I only looked at it as I walked past. The few extra blocks didn't take that much longer. One day, I sat on the bench for the bus stop, mentally re-created our walk through the house, and figured out which window was Latisha's bedroom. The southwest corner facing the bus shelter. And there were days I stood across the street, sat on the bench, or leaned against the bus shelter and simply watched the house.

About three weeks after our last conversation with Hanley and Morse, I stood at the bus stop and faced Latisha's room. I was thinking about a girl at school, Jan Everts, and replaying our conversation.

I had known Jan since sometime in the fifth grade when we had the same advanced reading class. We hadn't talked much, and I'm not sure we ever made eye contact. During middle school, we had more classes together and talked longer. Probably only a few seconds in reality.

After gym class, Jan had been standing in the hallway when I walked out of the locker room. She fell in step beside me as if she had been waiting for me and actually wanted to talk.

After a few seconds of how-are-yous, class comparisons, and relief the year would end soon, Jan expressed, "I hate all this running and sweating. You risk smelling bad, or you have to take an extra shower in the middle of the day. And with my crazy hair, I don't have enough time to calm it down again."

Jan's hair was brown, about shoulder-length, and looked like a combination of waves, curls, and frizz. It did look kind of crazy, and I couldn't imagine it calming down at all. Yet I was also at the age where I thought it would be fun to see how crazy her hair got with a slight electrical charge. I wondered if it would stand on end or maybe even dance.

"Yeah, it's a drag," I agreed. "It wasn't so bad last year when I had gym last hour. I could go home and not worry about being too gross."

"First hour might not be too bad," Jan suggested.

"I can see that. But this middle-of-the-day stuff, it sucks." I wasn't sure how to continue. Should I come up with a way of saying something nice? Compliment her hair, maybe? I wasn't sure I could, so I chose to babble. "At least we're in the tennis section now. I already play that, so I have an advantage, which I like. A lot of the class wouldn't play tennis if it wasn't required, which means I do okay against them. I get to run less."

"I'm in track and field," Jan told me. "Who does that outside of school?"

I shook my head.

"I mean, where would I use the shotput?" she asked. "How does the ability to stand on one foot, spin in a circle, and throw something heavy help me?"

I snickered. "Maybe doing transplants. You could shotput the heart into the open chest from across the room."

Jan laughed and wrinkled her nose. "That is so gross. Besides, I'd have to touch a heart."

"Yeah, that would be bad," I noted. "There's got to be something useful about gym class, though. Or any class, I would hope."

She stepped closer. The amount I was sweating increased sharply. I worried about smelling bad.

"I don't think I have tennis until we go back in the fall," Jan suggested. "You could teach me."

"But that would mean getting sweaty."

"That would be okay. I wouldn't mind. As long as it was with you, and you were getting sweaty at the same time."

As I stood at the bus stop, watching the bedroom window of a haunted house, I tried to figure out what actually happened. Did she really want to play tennis, or should I be nervous because she was getting me into something I didn't know anything about? Plus, what would make her do that?

A shadow moved across Latisha's bedroom window. It reminded me why I was there. When the curtains moved, I started to walk across the street. I focused on the window, looking for more movement, for the source of the shadow. A car screeched to a stop beside me, but I didn't care. I was focused on the window and walking when Linda Morse stepped in front of me and blocked my view.

"Daniels, are you okay?"

"What?" I tried to look past her. I stepped to the side, and she moved to stay in front of me.

"Daniels." She leaned over, almost yelling in my face. "Daniels, what's your problem?"

I quit trying to look around her and looked at her. "Oh, hi. Sorry. I was a little distracted."

"No, you were almost a little dead." She saw me again try to look past her. Her gaze followed mine. "What's the deal?"

"I saw movement in Latisha's window."

"Is that where we are?" Morse asked.

"Yeah."

She grabbed my arm and pulled me toward her car. "Stay close while I call Richard."

"Why?"

"We're not going in without him," Morse declared.

"You didn't know this was her family's house?"

"No, I didn't. If he's still coming over here and checking on the place, he's doing it on his time and without me."

"How did you know I was here?" I wondered.

"I didn't. We're riding solo, trying to get more cars on the streets. This is my regular cover area now. I was just driving by."

While Morse called Hanley, I stared out the window.

Thoughts of Jan Everts and tennis lessons flickered through my mind. I saw no further movement.

Hanley arrived within minutes and talked with Morse, after which they both moved their cars around to the alley. I watched. Obviously, they didn't intend to include me.

They opened the gate from the alley and started up the sidewalk. When Hanley opened the back screen door and reached for the doorknob, I told him, "It won't open."

Hanley scowled. "What are you doing here?"

"I'm the one who got you into this," I stated. "Do you actually think I'm going to wait by the car?"

"Yeah, I do."

"Well, this time, you're wrong."

"Why don't you think the door will open?" Morse asked.

I looked at her and shrugged. "Funny feeling."

Hanley reached out and tried the door. It was locked.

"Let's try the front door," I suggested.

He glared at me. "Why?"

"Funny feeling."

"I don't believe in them," he remarked.

"You don't have to."

Hanley let the screen door slam shut, and Morse inhaled sharply and cringed. He started walking around the house.

"Don't worry," I assured her. "There's nobody there to find out we're coming. At least, nobody that doesn't already know we're here." I shrugged. "At least nobody alive."

Her expression suggested she thought I had lost my mind. We started after Hanley.

By the time we caught up with him, he was already on the front porch, reaching for the doorknob. Morse and I held our breath as he turned it. The door wouldn't open. Hanley stepped back and looked as if he was getting ready to kick the door down.

"Wait. Let me try first."

He looked at me, then stepped back a few feet and waved me past.

I moved forward, grabbed the doorknob, and turned it. There was a *click*, and I pushed the door open.

"That's creepy," Morse intoned.

"It's impossible." Hanley pulled his gun and stepped toward the door. "How did you know it would open for you?" he asked.

"Funny feeling."

The corner of his mouth lifted. It wasn't quite a smile. "I still don't believe in them."

"I'm starting to." Morse sighed.

I stepped toward the door. Hanley set his fingers on my shoulder and stopped me. "You're never going to be able to follow instructions, are you?"

"Depends," I noted.

"Consider a stint in the military. It'll teach you to follow orders and give you a little discipline. Be good for you."

"Get me out of your hair, too, wouldn't it?" I commented.

Hanley nodded.

"Richard," Morse hissed. "What's wrong with you? Lighten up."

"Am I wrong?" he asked.

"Probably," Morse and I chorused.

At that, the three of us smiled, and the mood lightened.

I closed my eyes, listened, and inhaled deeply. "There's no threat here."

"How can you tell?" Morse asked.

"Another funny feeling." When Hanley rolled his eyes and slowly shook his head, I asked, "Can't you feel it?"

His eyes narrowed. Morse gave a little shrug.

"We're wanted here," I told them. "At least, I am."

"You're waiting by the car," Hanley insisted.

"Nope. Not on your life."

"Your mom will kill me if I let anything happen to you."

"There's no way I'm not going in."

"Fine. Don't say I didn't warn you," Hanley snapped. "But I'm leading the way."

"If you insist," I stated.

"Sounds like a lot of dominant male monkey stuff going on here," Morse claimed. "You two are not competing. We're working together. Got it?"

Hanley and I looked at each other. "Who's competing?" he asked.

"Certainly not me," I declared.

"Turn around and walk," Morse commanded. "Get through that door, and let's get this over with." Hanley turned and stepped into the house. I heard Morse add under her breath, "Kids." When I looked at her, she pointed at me, then flicked her hand, shooing me inside.

Inside, I headed straight for the stairs. We didn't need to look anywhere else. If Latisha wanted to show us something, her bedroom would be the most likely place.

"Daniels," Morse whisper-yelled. "You need to stay with us."

"Let's at least pretend we're following procedure," Hanley called. "Don't get us in trouble by running off and getting eaten."

I smiled, waved, and continued up the stairs. When I stepped into Latisha's bedroom, I immediately felt the cold, like last time. "She's in here," I remarked, and Morse and Hanley hustled up the stairs.

I stood in the middle of the room when Morse came through the door. She let out a "Brrr," and shivered as she passed through the cold spot.

Hanley followed her into the room and saw her shiver. "What was that?" he asked and took another step forward. "Geez. Cold. How does that happen?"

"Latisha was waiting there," I advised.

"You know, I felt a couple of chills when I was here before. And the afternoon I was looking for her. Just like that."

"That would have been her," I affirmed.

"Really?" Morse rejoined. "You expect me to…"

The closet door swung open.

I'd seen that trick already, so I watched Hanley and Morse. They stared with wide eyes. Hanley's gun was up and in front of him. Morse brought hers up to face the closet. When the door stopped moving partway open, then swung again until it was all the way open, they looked at each other.

From my spot, I could see into the closet. The hanging clothes were pushed to one end, and the shoe boxes of pictures sat on the floor. The bottom book of the stack on the shelf slid out and dropped onto the clothes rod, where it slid sideways until it hit a hanger, then banged to the floor. Even though we watched it, we all jumped. Latisha had new tricks for us.

Morse holstered her weapon, picked up the book, and examined it. She turned it toward Hanley and me. It was Latisha's yearbook.

"Any chance the killer is someone at her school?" Morse wondered.

Before we could say anything, the book was ripped from Morse's hands and thrown to the bed. "Sweet Jesus." Morse stepped back. "Is it her? Is it Latisha?"

Hanley's pointed his gun at the book and sidestepped.

"Yeah, it is," I proclaimed.

"Is she pissed?" Morse asked. "Why is she pissed at us? We're on her side."

"I don't think she's mad at us."

"If I believed in ghosts, I'd probably agree," Hanley commented.

The yearbook flipped open. Hanley lowered his weapon as the three of us moved closer to the bed. "There she is," Morse pointed out. Latisha's picture was at the end of the second row.

Pages flipped and stopped at one with pictures of small groups of kids being themselves. Latisha was in the middle of the page with a wide smile and shining eyes.

"It isn't anybody she went to school with. We have our guy," I insisted. "I think she wants us to know her better. She's trying to make proving who her killer is personal to us all."

"How do you know that?" Hanley demanded. I only looked at him until he answered himself. "You and your funny feelings are going to be a pain in my backside for a long time. I can just tell."

"Having funny feelings of your own?" I asked.

"Nothing funny about it."

The yearbook lifted off the bed, rose to about the height of my chin, and began to spin in a circle. "The trouble is that it's already personal," Hanley revealed. He wasn't talking to Morse or me. He was addressing the room and whoever else was in it. "Has been since before I found you. Since before I met your mom and she gave me your picture. We believe we have the man who attacked you, but we haven't proven it yet. So, believe me, it's still personal."

The yearbook dropped to the bed. Hanley turned and looked at me. "I guess I have to thank you and Latisha for making sure I have another chance to do this right. Let's do everything we can to prove we have our killer and get him put away forever."

I shrugged as if helping in some bizarre way was a thing I did all the time, then moved to the dresser. I returned the picture of Latisha I'd borrowed on my first visit and had been carrying in my backpack since.

CHAPTER THIRTY-SIX

<u>June 2001</u>

Against my better judgment, I started summer vacation by agreeing to teach Jan Everts tennis. She didn't catch on like John, Warren, and Rachel had, but I'm not sure she was trying too hard. We had a lot of laughs and got to be close while I taught her how to hold and swing the racquet. Jan always smelled delicious and was warm to the touch. Being with her was interesting and complicated. About what I expected. Most of the time, I was never really sure what I was supposed to do.

Tennis quickly became an excuse. We'd sit on the bench, where we talked and watched other people play. I tried to keep some space between us, but it was more difficult every day. After we spent a few evenings just hanging, we dropped the tennis pretense altogether.

Our days became regular social events. John, Warren, and a couple of Jan's female friends frequently joined us. We took in a few movies, laughed our way through some lanes of bowling, or hung out somewhere, like our house or the park. I came to anticipate the evenings when I had Jan to myself.

Prior to hanging with me, Jan had always been part of a large mixed crowd. Her popularity was one of the reasons I was surprised when she approached me for tennis lessons. She could have asked anybody, including the people actually on the team. I knew she had boyfriends in the past but not who or how many. Nor did I really care.

I considered asking her, "why me," then thought better of it. I was enjoying us and didn't want my curiosity to get her wondering the same thing and lead her to move on. If she had a reason to seek me out, she never said.

One Friday evening, we were shooting pool at our favorite hamburger joint when I met one of her exes, a football player named Chris. I stood beside Jan, watching Warren line up his shot when Chris appeared behind me and threw a punch to the side of my head, just behind my ear. I went down, rolled away, and came back to my feet, facing him.

Chris was a year older than us and had already moved on to high school. He was taller than John and probably weighed what John, Jan, and I did combined. I suspected he started on steroids so he could compete with the older football players.

"Is this why you won't go with me anymore?" Chris asked Jan, pointing at me.

"No," she told him quietly.

Warren made the mistake of stepping between Chris and me. "Hey, asshole, you can't come in here and do that!"

Chris dropped Warren with a right jab to the chin.

Jan stepped forward and grabbed Chris' arm. "Chris, stop."

He pushed her away, and her legs tangled with Warren. She fell back against the pool table and landed on the floor, sprawled across Warren.

I looked at Chris and shook my head. "You know, I would have let you have the shot at me," I stated. "Forgiven and forgotten. Sort of." I smiled at him. "You shouldn't have involved my friends, though. You shouldn't have hit anybody else."

John had circled the pool table. I originally thought it was to make sure he was out of harm's way. Then I saw him pull a pool cue back for a good swing. Fortunately, he looked in my direction before swinging for the fence. With a twitch and a glance, I warned him off. He lowered the cue and backed away a few steps.

Chris hadn't had enough yet. He threw a big round-house punch at my face. People seem to like throwing roundhouses at me. I leaned to the side and back, watching it sweep past me. As my smile broadened, his confidence faded. He had expected the beating to be over already.

In my best Bert Lahr, which was lousy, I drawled, "C'mooooon. Try again."

He responded with a jab, a much better choice. I used my left hand to deflect it and hit his chin with the heel of my right hand. Chris wobbled and stumbled back.

He tried another punch, and I kicked him in the stomach.

The wind rushing from his lungs was audible over the

too-loud sound system and the noisy people who hadn't noticed Chris and I were having a discussion. He tried to swallow air, to gasp a breath. I stepped aside and kicked him behind the knee, dropping him to the floor as he continued gasping. Unlike Rachel's assailants in the past, after Chris regained his breath, he'd be okay except for a bruise or two and a battered ego.

That was when I noticed Hanley and Morse sharing a table and watching quietly from the other side of the half-wall that separated the pool tables from the dining room. They were out of uniform, and burgers and bottles of beer sat between them.

Morse was almost smiling. Hanley was not.

As they threw down their napkins and made their way toward the altercation, I kept an eye on Chris and helped Warren and Jan to their feet. I draped an arm around Jan and looked at Warren. "That wasn't too bright. You've never been much of a fighter."

He smiled as he rubbed his chin. "It seemed like the right thing to do at the time." He stopped rubbing, looked at Jan, and stood straighter. "Always willing to help the ladies."

I could feel Jan smiling at him. I patted his shoulder. "Thanks, man. I appreciate it. I always know you've got my back, especially if a lady is close."

"Always," Warren agreed. "Especially then."

I turned to Jan. "Are you okay?"

She nodded. "That's why I wouldn't go with him anymore. He is possessive and controlling and…and has a horrible temper."

We both watched Chris as Hanley lifted him to his feet.

Morse held her badge in front of his nose. Chris still seemed to be having trouble catching his breath but focused on the badge okay.

"We saw the whole thing," Morse claimed. "Looked like a bully assaulting three younger kids. To me, it appeared they were defending themselves."

Chris looked from her to Hanley, who still had a pretty good grip on him.

"If you promise to go home and leave these kids alone from now on, we won't press the assault charges," Hanley announced.

Chris nodded, and Hanley released his grip. "Good. You're capable of learning."

Chris slunk away, unable to look Jan in the eyes. She turned to Morse and Hanley. "Thank you. I'm glad you were here."

"We seem to be seeing a lot of each other," I remarked. "Are you watching us?"

"Of course not," Morse countered.

"Why would we do that?" Hanley inquired.

"Then it must be a coincidence." Their expressions suggested I'd said what they wanted me to believe. "Not that I actually believe in coincidences," I added.

They shared a quick glance. "Kids aren't the only ones who know where to get a good burger," Morse blurted. I stared at her, and she continued. "Cops know all the best places. Really."

Hanley tried to stare a few holes in my head. "You seemed to enjoy that little battle."

"Why would you think that?"

"You were smiling," he pointed out.

I shook my head. "Violence should be the last resort, not a first step. Some situations, some people, leave you with no choice."

"You were still smiling," Hanley insisted.

"Must be something subconscious I do to offset the tension," I declared. "Something to create doubt."

"Sure," Hanley drawled. "That must be it."

"How long have you been studying martial arts?" Morse asked.

"Six or seven years. How could you tell?"

"You didn't have to do much. Also, some of the moves looked familiar, like we might be studying the same style," Morse suggested. "Your technique seemed pretty good. What got you into it?"

"Mom thought it would be a good idea. Thought I could use a little discipline, a way to release energy," I explained. "She also thought, since my dad died when I was so young, that I could use some male influence. Rather than get a boyfriend or something worse, she signed me up with the guy who runs his school in one of the buildings she owns."

"Turns out your mom was right," Morse noted. "She's a sharp lady."

I smiled and nodded.

"So, do you compete?" she asked.

"Nah. Not really interested in that."

"Well, then. What belt are you?"

"I don't know. I've never tested."

"Really? What does your sensei say?" Morse challenged.

"He's disappointed in me as a whole. He agrees with me that a fancy uniform isn't important, but he doesn't think I try hard enough. He says I could be good, a natural, if only I had some discipline."

"So, try harder. Try a competition. You'll be amazed how much more you can get out of it," she recommended.

"I'm not competitive, though. I don't find much pleasure in beating someone—"

"Could've fooled me," Hanley cut in.

"—at something," I finished. "I only compete with myself. See how much better I can do than the last time."

"Then you should try Forms," Morse offered. "It's all about technique, skill, and style. You compete, but it's really against yourself. I'm competing in a match this weekend at the Minneapolis Convention Center. Why don't you come and see what it's all about?"

"Yeah, maybe," I proposed. "We'll have to see."

Jan grabbed my arm and bounced. "It could be fun. I'd like to see it."

Hanley and Morse returned to their table and sat back down.

"I think we should probably move on," I stated.

"Really?" Warren asked. "After that, I think I can win this game."

Jan turned to me. "You okay?"

"Not really," I admitted. "I should probably take you home." I had no idea why, but it seemed like the best thing we could do.

"Warren and I will finish the game, then head out," John remarked. "We'll be fine. You two go ahead and split."

I got a couple of to-go boxes, and we packed up the rest of our burgers. Warren was lining up a shot, but John watched us leave. We walked past Hanley and Morse. "Thanks for your help," I told them.

"Any time," Hanley replied. "Just be careful."

"See you at the Convention Center," Morse stated.

"I'm looking forward to it," Jan returned.

Without saying a word, I somehow felt committed. I wasn't sure I liked it.

CHAPTER THIRTY-SEVEN

Jan and I stuck to the sidewalks and made sure we passed beneath the streetlights as I walked her home. My discomfort had not decreased. Jan took my hand as we turned up the sidewalk to her house. She pulled me around to the side, into the shadows of the overhangs. She stepped in front of me, moved closer, and placed her hands on my chest.

"I really like hanging out with you," she told me. "I've had a lot of fun."

"Yeah. I've enjoyed it, too."

"I like how you tried not to hurt Chris. I mean, he's a jerk, but …"

"It's okay. I'd prefer not to hurt anyone too bad, and I've learned to be more careful about who needs it. Especially if the police are sitting there."

"Did you know they were there?" Jan questioned.

"No," I declared. "I didn't have a clue."

"Anyway, I'm glad you didn't hurt him. And you made

me feel really safe. Especially when you put your arm around me afterward."

I shrugged.

"You do realize that's the first time you've touched me like that, actually held me, don't you?"

"No," I admitted. "Again, I don't have a clue." I brought my hands up and put them on her sides. I felt her ribcage expand as she inhaled. She might have been right, which meant this was the second intimate gesture I'd made while we'd been hanging out. On the other hand, Jan had made quite a bit of physical contact. She'd touched my hands, arms, legs, shoulders, and even my face at various points. I was pretty sure I remembered them all.

She leaned forward and kissed me, her eyes closed, her lips moist.

Suddenly, I once again worried about sweating and smelling bad. Her lips lingered on mine for a few seconds, then moved away. Mine remained where they were. After I reminded myself to breathe, I blinked.

"Is it okay that I did that?" Jan asked.

"Sure." It came out as a whisper. I'm not sure I had the strength or the air for more.

She leaned in again. This time, my lips moved in response to hers. I was relieved they'd developed a mind of their own. I did think enough to tell my eyes to close, just in case she opened hers. I didn't want her to see the fear in them.

We stood in the shadows and kissed for a while. I found myself enjoying the contact, the pressure and sensation. In the middle, I wondered if something told me this was coming. Maybe that was the reason I felt uncomfortable after our altercation with Chris. Some fear of the unknown or unwitting performance anxiety. It seemed ridiculous since I didn't know I would be performing something.

Jan called early the next morning. She had arranged a ride for us to the Convention Center so we could watch the martial arts competitions. We saw Linda Morse compete soon after we arrived. When the competitors did Forms, they went through a series of moves that demonstrated speed, kick height, fluidity, mastery, and skills. Based on my limited knowledge, I thought Morse did really well. Jan said it looked like a ballet. Unfortunately, Morse did not move up to the next level of competition.

We found her after she finished and talked for a while. I didn't see Hanley anywhere around. Either he was working, or I had misjudged the nature of their relationship. Or he didn't like to watch martial arts competitions.

Morse introduced us to her instructor, a woman named Mia, who was about my mom's size and age with short, curly hair. I could tell Jan was intrigued. She talked about signing up for a basic self-defense course. When Morse told Mia I was also studying, she asked who my teacher was. I told her Mr. Lee at Martial Living, and she said I was lucky. That he was an excellent teacher and a master at multiple forms but selective in who he took on as students. She said she'd love to work with him sometime and that she could learn a lot from someone like him. I told her I'd convey the message and took her business card.

Jan and I watched the competition for a while longer. One group competed in Combat and Weapons, where they scored points by making a clean hit on their opponent. In Combat, they mostly used hands and feet. But in Weapons, they used swords, nunchucks, and other fun things I'd never played with in my lessons. I realized there were a lot of techniques and methods I hadn't learned yet. Most likely due to my attitude. As I considered what Mia had said about Mr. Lee, I understood what an opportunity I had. A reason to work hard and benefit from someone who'd been in my life for a while and suspected I had more in me.

I was on a mission.

CHAPTER THIRTY-EIGHT

<u>September 2001</u>

The return to school meant a return to rituals. We planned to meet by the front door of Patrick Henry High School, where I was now a freshman, and go to the Camden area branch of the Minneapolis Public Library. We'd hang out and pretend to do homework there.

Except a feeling more ominous than anything I could remember in a long time overtook me. Something was going to happen, or I was supposed to be someplace I didn't want to go.

It didn't matter. I just knew I shouldn't be with Jan, John, Warren, or anyone else who planned on joining us. I shouldn't lead them into whatever was supposed to happen.

Instead of going toward the door, I saw Jan near her locker and crept up behind her. "Hey, cute stuff," I whispered.

Without turning around, Jan remarked, "Hello, liar."

I knew a smile played on her lips. Lips that I enjoyed

kissing often and intensely, now that I'd started. Jan was convinced she wasn't beautiful or even cute. Maybe she wasn't a perfect physical specimen, model material, or even in Rachel Thompson's league, but it didn't matter to me. Or to any of the other guys who seemed to flock in constant pursuit, waiting for her to get tired of me.

Jan was a little taller than me, even though she was one of the shortest girls at school. I still hoped to grow a bit. I expected that to happen later. She had wide hips and was a bit knock-kneed, long on torso and short on leg. Plus, that crazy hair I loved to tease her about, telling her it moved and coiled as I watched. That I was afraid to run my fingers through it because I might not get them back. Even if she did call me a liar, I had made it clear I appreciated her and her looks. And like everyone else, she had to appreciate a sincere, well-intentioned compliment.

"What's going on?" she asked. "I thought we were meeting by the door. Isn't the whole gang going to the library?"

I tried to look apologetic. "I'm not able to go. I got a message from Mom. Something has come up, and she needs me to go home."

"Is everything okay?"

"Yeah. I think she wants me to keep the carpet cleaners company or something like that."

"I can go to the library any time. It's not like I'm looking for anything. You want me to go with you?"

"Of course I do, but no," I told her. "Go hang out, have some fun. It'll be boring with me. If it's the carpet cleaners, we won't even be able to walk around the house. Can't leave footprints. I'll call you after a while."

"Are you sure?"

"Yeah. I'll see you later."

Jan leaned over and kissed me. "Okay, but it's your loss."

A public display right in the middle of the school. Another first for me. I didn't know if it was for her, but it didn't matter. I wanted to continue. I thought about changing my mind, maintaining the story, and letting her come home with me even though the carpet cleaners wouldn't show so I could kiss her some more. Instead, I watched her walk away.

I headed out from the opposite end of the building from where we were supposed to meet. It was in the general direction of home and pointed directly toward the house occupied by the ghost of Latisha Ford.

I stuck to the sidewalks and major streets as much as I could. I was less than a block from school when I knew I was being watched and followed. I tried to casually look around, checking to see if anyone was looking at me but didn't see anybody. I stopped and tied my shoe, then examined a piece of paper lying along the curb, which I threw in the nearest wastebasket. I kicked a few rocks at the storm sewer. All in hopes of seeing movement or a shadow. I stopped in front of a barber shop and again at a dog groomer, pretending to be looking inside while I actually watched the reflections in the windows. Whoever watched and followed me was excellent at being invisible.

I stood at the bus stop across the street from Latisha's home for a few minutes and watched the house. I still felt the person watching me, but I couldn't tell where from. Convinced my watcher wasn't going to leave, I crossed the street to the house. I went through the gate, up the sidewalk, and in the unlocked front door. After locking it behind me, I crept up to Latisha's room and peeked out the window.

And saw nobody.

From the windows in her bedroom, I could view the two streets making up their corner and most of the front and side yards. The alley was blocked from view. I moved between the two windows, stuck to the shadows, or crawled along the floor, staying out of sight as much as possible. I tried not to cast a shadow like the one that had brought Hanley, Morse, and me into the house. As the sun moved west and the shadows lengthened, it became easier to move around without worry.

Someone waited outside, out of sight. No matter how good they were at being invisible, though, they couldn't escape my ability to feel their presence. Maybe I did have some talent I could appreciate.

Based on the increase in traffic and the number of Metro Transit buses passing by, rush hour had begun. It was late enough that I needed to get home, but I hesitated.

When rush hour was over, and dusk approached, I snuck out the back door. Between the neighbor's fence and the corner of the Fords' garage was an opening big enough for a medium-sized dog. I slipped through it and into the neighbor's yard. After crawling through a hole in their hedge, I ran down the alley, heading away from all the places I wanted to be.

I was a couple of blocks from Latisha's home, backtracking toward school, when I realized I was no longer being watched and hadn't been since leaving Latisha's.

That was when a police car pulled up next to me.

Morse powered down her window and called me over. As I got close, she slipped it into park. Something passed between her and Hanley in the passenger seat. They got out of the car, and the three of us stood beneath the street-light and stared at each other for a minute.

When you're staring down the police, even though you believe you've done nothing wrong, a minute can be a long time.

Finally, I asked, "Are you guys being social, or did I do something wrong that I'm not aware of? Something I should have enjoyed more?"

Hanley shook his head. "Don't know how to be social."

Morse made a sound that may have been a laugh. "Understatement," she muttered. Maybe it had been a snort of frustration or disgust.

"So," I drawled. "What's wrong?"

"Martin Franklin has escaped," Morse stated.

I only looked at them. I knew what I had been feeling. Martin Franklin was my tail. Somehow, he knew where I went to school, what time my day ended, and he was waiting for me. I wasn't sure what to say, how to tell them what I knew or thought I knew, so I kept quiet.

I also had no idea why, if he intended to do something, he didn't do it while I walked to Latisha's. Why he didn't follow me into the house and do it there. Maybe he'd lasted as long as he had by being careful.

The silence between the three of us was tangible. Like high Minnesota humidity, it hung in the cooling air. You could feel it long before it congealed into fog.

Hanley finally broke the silence. "Bastard killed three

people when he escaped. Two from the prison and a Hennepin County Sheriff's deputy."

More silence.

Finally, I decided to share a comment I knew they didn't want to hear. "And now, he's coming after me."

They shuffled me into the car and started driving in the general direction of my home. We were all silent for a few minutes.

"So. How did it happen?" I asked.

Morse adjusted the mirror so she could see me as she drove. The streetlights cast blocks of light into the car when we passed beneath them. Hanley turned in his seat until he could see me.

"The prison guards brought him to the Hennepin County Courthouse," Morse explained. "The county was going to arraign Franklin for Latisha Ford's murder and maybe one other. Richard and I talked a lot about the questions you asked the day you found us at the range. We got the right people looking at things, trying to find answers."

Hanley continued. "With what we found, and thanks to the availability of the physical and DNA evidence we got during Rachel Thompson's investigation, we put together a solid case against Franklin."

"But there's more," Morse revealed.

"Yeah," Hanley agreed. "We've been holding out on you, helping you stay a kid."

"You sound like one, too," Morse declared. "Nana-nana-boo-boo, we know something you don't." Her tone was that of a mocking little girl.

"I didn't say it like that," Hanley professed.

"Damn near," Morse quipped.

I stuck my tongue out and made a raspberry noise, and we all laughed.

"Damn kids," Morse grumbled. "How can you joke at a time like this?"

"If you can't laugh, you'll go nuts," I stated.

"How old are you?" Hanley asked.

"I don't know. I'd have to do the math."

"For someone who can't count very high, you keep coming up with some deep shit," Hanley contended. "Almost philosophical."

"So what else do you know that I don't?" I asked. "Obviously not philosophy."

"No, I never got past the Star Trek logic and ethics," Hanley admitted. "All that heavy thinking is for the serious types. Like Linda. She took that stuff in college."

"Yeah," Morse replied. "He took bowling."

"And badminton. And sculpture. I got an A." He gloated for a moment.

"So you found something in the cemetery," I suggested.

"We followed the course of action we had discussed at the ice cream shop," Morse agreed. "The cemetery management was very helpful, provided us with a complete schedule of burials and services, both on the grounds and in the buildings."

"Going back fifteen years, we found six disappearances within a day or two of a burial," Hanley remarked. "With that much time, it could have been a coincidence. Except John picked out five of the six girls who went missing from our stack of pictures the afternoon we were together."

"So he buried six in the cemetery and was going back to bury Latisha when he could. If you hadn't found her," I surmised. "That would be a girl in our cemetery about every two years."

"That's what we figured, too," Morse confirmed. "On average, a killing every two years."

"But he took Rachel a long way from that cemetery," I pointed out.

"Which probably means he has another dump site," Hanley stated.

"Is there a cemetery close to where I found Rachel?"

"I don't know," Morse declared. "Not off the top of my head. We're going to check that out, too."

"But if he had another dump site, he probably wasn't waiting two years between killings," I announced. "We need to keep digging if we're going to find them all."

"I agree," Hanley added. "We've got a lot more to do."

"But we got their attention," Morse pointed out. "It's going to be easier going forward."

"With the information from one cemetery, we had enough to get the bosses to talk to the University of Minnesota about underground radar," Hanley explained. "They sent us to the University of Montana, who was using one on a mammoth dig. The professor and an assistant drove to Minneapolis so we could try it."

"Did you tell them how you came up with this plan?" I asked. "That ghosts were insisting you do this?"

"We have one lieutenant who's seen enough odd things through the years that we figured he'd be open-minded enough to hear the truth," Morse revealed. "He was, and it stayed with him."

"The others were only told about the data and the suspicion as to why Latisha had been buried in the brush pile," Hanley stated. "I made it sound like I came up with the idea in case it was written off as crazy."

Morse nodded. "One of the graves we wanted them to look at was close to Rachel's. One of the many in the Anderson section."

"I may know that grave," I told them.

They looked at me funny but knew better than to ask.

Hanley continued. "So they set this thing up, turned it on, and set it off. And in the image that came up on the screen were two skulls, one behind the other."

"The casket metal didn't block the signal?" I asked.

"No, at least not this time," Hanley remarked. "The professor said if the metal blocked the signal, we wouldn't see what was in the casket, but we might still see what was beneath depending on the angles and refraction."

"Things can happen fast when they need to," Morse pointed out. "One of the lieutenants called a couple of the commanders out to the site. One of *them* called an inspector, who called a judge, while the other got a number from cemetery management and called the Anderson family. They all converged on the cemetery. We received permission to exhume the grave at the same time we received the warrant to dig up the cemetery if need be."

"It was like you predicted," Hanley declared. "Beneath the casket was a skeleton."

Morse picked it back up. "Forensics went to work on it. They assembled the skeleton and did a reconstruction of the face. They were able to determine she was about your age when she died. They compared her teeth to existing dental records, and we found a match."

"They also sifted through the dirt in and around the grave," Hanley added.

"They found Girl Scout badges, didn't they?" I asked.

"Yeah. Is that from one of your funny feelings?"

"That, too," I confirmed. "The girl John described as being our age was a Girl Scout. Considering what he saw as he looked at her, it only made sense she would be one of the girls in that cemetery for sure."

"Okay, that makes sense. I like it better than all these feelings you rely on, but it did give us more we could use for a positive identification. Her name was Roxanne Delaney."

Hanley jumped in. "They also found a piece of rope beneath the casket. Evidently, he used nylon rope on Roxanne, and nylon decays slower than natural fibers."

"Considering it was still tied around her skeleton's neck, that gave us his method of killing, as it had the other two we know of," Morse stated.

"It gave the bosses enough circumstantial evidence that they were considering charging Franklin with her murder, too," Hanley expounded.

"Good. I'm glad it worked out. I'm sure Latisha and her family and Roxanne and her family will be relieved." I looked at Hanley. "Do you believe in capital punishment?"

His eyes held mine for a few long seconds before he answered, "Some days I do."

"Me, too."

"What brought that up?" Morse inquired. "We don't have capital punishment in Minnesota."

"I know. We've been talking about it in school." I drew a deep breath. "What about evil? Do you believe in evil?"

"That's a tough one, too," Hanley professed. "Mostly, I think people make bad choices, then try to cover it up. Usually by making more bad choices. It keeps getting worse until they have no choice but to do stupid things."

"Sometimes I believe in evil," Morse declared. "When I see what people are capable of doing to each other."

"It exists," I claimed. "I first saw it when I looked into Martin Franklin's eyes. I've become convinced it's around us." I looked at them both, then out the window. "I'm sorry. We got off on a tangent. I want to hear the rest of Franklin's escape."

They looked at each other. I was unable to read their expressions. It may have been fear or bewilderment. Or concern for my sanity.

"After they got him to the courthouse, Franklin needed to use a restroom," Morse explained. "Before they could get him re-secured, he overpowered the guards. Then he killed a deputy sheriff, who happened to come into the restroom at the wrong time. Franklin left the building wearing the deputy's clothes and carrying his gun."

Hanley watched me as we drove in silence. I spent most of the rest of the way home looking out the car window, wondering where Martin Franklin was hiding. Wondering why I could feel him earlier but couldn't now. Had he gotten bored or decided he lost me and went home, wherever that was?

As we pulled to the curb in front of my house, I repeated, "Now, he's coming after me."

Morse put the car in park. Hanley turned all the way around to face me. "You've said that twice now. Why do you think that?"

"Funny feeling."

He snorted a laugh. "I should have seen that one coming."

"You do know that the day he was sentenced for Rachel's killing, he told me he'd see me soon, don't you?"

Their wide-open eyes told me I must have forgotten to tell them that part.

"I remember that day," Hanley recalled. "You were looking at Franklin and said, 'I'll be ready.' Is that why you said it?"

"Must have been." I shrugged. I didn't remember saying I'd be ready. "Well, I could feel something this afternoon. Like I was being watched. Like something was going to happen."

I looked from Hanley to Morse. They looked back at me, and I saw their concern. I felt something else, but I couldn't be certain what it was.

Then it came out. "Franklin has been looking for an opportunity to escape since we first busted him," Hanley admitted.

Morse nodded. "It appears that way. Out for a little vengeance. We handed him the perfect chance by turning his next arraignment into some huge public spectacle."

"He played the system," Hanley put in.

"So what do we do now?" Morse wondered.

It was my turn to laugh. Or snort. "Find him?" I suggested.

"We're working on it," Hanley countered. "Finding an escaped serial killer is a bit of a priority." His sarcasm came through in his tone.

"I know. Besides the anger and pain from losing those men, it must be embarrassing to have him loose."

"If you recall, he was homeless and transient," Morse stated. "There aren't many places he can hide. He's probably moved out of the area. Or gone to ground, hiding somewhere he feels safe. He'll likely never come near you. He'll turn up somewhere else."

"Or make us flip every rock and rotted tree looking for him," Hanley remarked.

"No. He's still around. He's coming," I insisted. "You may not think it, but I know it. In fact, I'm counting on it." I looked from one to the other. "And I'm counting on you to be there."

Hanley wiped a hand across his face and suddenly looked tired. Morse released a big sigh, then nodded.

"How many of the guys he killed today did you know?" I asked.

"Two," Hanley stated.

"Were you close?"

"The deputy sheriff was in some of my classes back in college."

"One of the two guards he killed actually used to be a Minneapolis cop," Morse added. "He had a case he couldn't break, and it haunted him…"

"Kind of like Latisha and me," Hanley declared.

"He decided he didn't need the stress and retired to being a guard at Oak Park Heights."

"I really am sorry," I offered. "Franklin has killed too many. And too close." We all sat quietly for a moment. "Couldn't they have had the arraignment at the prison?" I asked.

Hanley shrugged. "Probably, but it was a high-profile case and would have been a high-profile trial. They wanted to make a spectacle of it. Decided the day after the Labor Day holiday was perfect."

"Why? What made this case so special?"

"Latisha died, and her case went cold at a time when the force was being accused of indifference to crimes against minority victims," Morse revealed.

"So it didn't sit well that we weren't able to solve her murder quickly," Hanley expounded.

Morse vaguely gestured. "And if they chose to indict him for Roxanne Delaney's murder, too, it would have been even better. Proof that the force never gave up on finding justice for a victim, no matter how long it took."

"It doesn't matter to you who or what the victim is, does it?" I inquired.

Hanley shook his head.

"You try not to let it get personal, but in actuality, it is. You try to take care of all the victims, don't you?"

He nodded. "Yeah."

"And you're pretty much the same way?" I asked Morse.

"Pretty much," she agreed.

"I think it's okay. The world, the innocent, needs someone watching out for them. And the bad guys need something to be afraid of. I can't think of two better people to do the job."

They almost looked embarrassed.

"Stop me before I say something nice," I quipped.

That got them to smile.

"We really don't know how many Martin Franklin has

killed," I contended. "We don't know where he's been, where he's lived, what kind of friends he may have."

"You're right," Hanley agreed. "We've been trying to recreate his life, but he's been no help. He won't tell us anything and hasn't left much of a trail. It doesn't help that Rachel and Latisha don't fit into any easy-to-see pattern. And his friends, or network or whatever you want to call them, aren't telling us anything, either. They've closed ranks. Not that there are many to talk to."

"You mean the people who live on the streets would rather protect a serial killer than get blamed or involved themselves?"

"Apparently," Hanley intoned. "No one wants to snitch on one of their own."

"Not to mention, most of them haven't had good experiences with the police. They tend not to trust," Morse remarked.

"I keep trying to figure out what motivates a person like him. It's beyond my comprehension," I admitted.

Hanley smirked. "I feel that way a lot of days, too."

"Some serial killers are after notoriety," Morse offered. "Trying to ensure their place in history. After they're caught, they'll tell investigators just about anything. Especially if it will help in their quest for fame."

"Trying to get on TV and in the movies," Hanley mused.

"So, what, Franklin isn't after the fame?" I asked. "He just enjoys the killing?"

They both shrugged. "Could be," Morse commented.

"Then we need to find him before he creates any more victims," I declared.

"You're right, Daniels," Hanley noted. "Finding him is an imperative."

"Do you have a plan?" Morse asked. "Some ideas? Something you should be sharing before you get out of the way and stay there?"

"We don't know enough about him or his victims to create a good profile," I stated.

"Right. There isn't enough information."

"Plus, he's free and in town, looking for me. We probably don't have time to work backward, start at the victims we know, and try to analyze him from there."

"We probably don't have enough victims to try that," Hanley remarked.

"You forget we have more than we're indicting him for," I pointed out. "Remember the ones John identified, too."

"If we include Latisha and Rachel, we're up to seven we know about," Morse recalled. "That is better."

"But we don't know if Franklin killed the others," Hanley rebutted.

"Maybe you don't know it, but I do. Then again, knowing isn't proving, is it?"

Morse raised an eyebrow. "You may be on to something, Daniels. Let's look at what we do know. Race, hair, and eye color don't matter to him. The victims appear to be between ten and sixteen, maybe seventeen years old. He's willing to keep them alive for a few days, like it appears he did with Rachel, or kill them quickly like he did Latisha. He likes to give them a proper burial where he thinks they'll be left untouched and undiscovered."

"And he's been right," Hanley noted. "We haven't found most of them."

"Did you ever get the work records from the cemetery?" I asked.

"If we did, somebody else is working them. We'll check on it again. See if his name is on there. See if he left an address we can investigate."

"Since we know nothing about him, we've been guessing he's homeless and transient because he looks it," I suggested. "Have we checked missing person reports along the bus and train routes in and out of Minnesota?"

Hanley shook his head. "I don't think we considered it possible that a homeless person could make their way around the country."

"You're right, Daniels," Morse replied. "We need to expand our search."

"And look at cemeteries close to the tracks and bus routes," I urged. "Since he went for so many years without being caught, he could have been confident enough to snatch a girl under everybody's nose any time he wanted."

"God, there's got to be another way to find this creep," Morse declared.

"Well, you could start by being there when he comes for me," I suggested.

"Should we take you and your mom into protective custody?" Morse asked.

"No. Then he'd only go after everybody else we know."

"Should we talk to his mom and get him grounded?" Hanley wondered.

Morse snickered. "That would probably be worse and more confining than protective custody, wouldn't it?"

"I can't believe you two. I haven't said anything about having a plan or that I wanted to be involved, or even that I was going to do something stupid." I glared at them. "I think you're taking this to an extreme."

"Maybe," Hanley demurred. "But we're enjoying it."

"Make a deal with you," Morse offered. "You let us handle this, and we won't say anything to alarm your mom. If you come up with any thoughts that may help, you call us. You will not act upon them. You will not do anything on your own. Agreed?"

"Okay. Fine. We'll do it your way." It was easier to go along, even if it went against everything I believed.

CHAPTER THIRTY-NINE

The next day, my nerves were on edge, like I was unprepared for a dreaded test. I couldn't say it was anything specific, though. I walked out the front door of the school with the group and knew someone was waiting. "You know, I'm not feeling the best," I remarked. "I think I better go home."

"You've been acting a little peculiar today," Jan pointed out.

"He's always peculiar," John stated. "But yes, he's off, even for Daniels."

"I'll call you guys later." I turned and went back inside the school. I felt extra eyes on me as I moved to the shadows inside the door. I hoped they and the reflections on the glass would help make me invisible. Jan and John kept looking in my direction as they followed Warren and a couple of Jan's friends down the sidewalk

But it was the other set of eyes I was most worried about. I hoped the few seconds we were together outside did not put Jan, John, and Warren in danger. I was beginning to resent Martin Franklin's intrusion into my life. Not only would I not get to be with Jan, but I didn't even get a kiss when I left.

After the gang was gone, I stepped out the front door and stood in the sun. I knew it was Franklin's presence I felt. I tried to casually examine the neighborhood but didn't see him anywhere. I couldn't decide. If I had seen him, would I have called the police or gone after him? Maybe it was a good thing he hid well.

I selected different streets and different shops with reflective windows as I made my way to Latisha's home. Even with extra rock-kicking and shoe-tying, I couldn't find my shadow. I stood at the bus stop for a few minutes again, then approached the house and let myself in the front door. I had been conscientious about locking it the night before, but it was open again. Latisha was still working with me.

I kept vigil as I had the day before, moving in the shadows between the windows, but I still couldn't find Franklin.

Dark had settled when I let myself out and headed home by a different route yet again. By then, I could feel he'd wandered off.

I wished I hadn't told Mom what was going on.

I checked in with Jan and John but didn't tell them anything. Their knowing didn't seem like a good idea. On the other hand, I couldn't decide if not warning them would protect them or put them in jeopardy.

The next day, I told them I still wasn't feeling well and left school early before they could catch up and ask what was wrong. Even before I made it out of the building, I knew Martin Franklin watched and waited.

I found a third route to Latisha's home. This time, I didn't linger at the bus stop. I simply went in the front door and up the stairs. Another session of watching did not reveal Franklin. After dark, I took a third route home.

I called Warren and John and asked them to meet me at Jan's house that evening. After telling Mom where I was going, I took out the trash, let myself out of the house, and disappeared down the alley. I snuck over to Jan's, being careful not to let anyone see me. I didn't feel I was being followed.

My plan brought me to Jan's a few minutes early. From the shadows of her garage, I watched the neighborhood until John and Warren arrived, then waited a few minutes more. When I was convinced they weren't being followed and I was alone, I snuck to the door.

John and Warren thought we were going to work on homework. We all had something in one of our classes we were struggling with, and being at Jan's provided an opportunity to get some help and have a few laughs. Plus, her parents weren't home.

Jan let me inside. I quickly closed the door, shut off the inside and outside lights, and looked out the window.

"Daniels, what's going on?" John demanded. "Where are your books?" He noticed my dark clothing. "We're not here for homework, are we?"

I shook my head.

He faced me, hands on his hips, and tried to look tough. He only looked tall and skinny, though. "You've been a little off the last few days. Not yourself. Remember, we said you were peculiar. Care to explain?"

"What do you mean, 'a little off'?" Jan asked.

"Distant, preoccupied," Warren listed. "Since you've come around, he's been staying away from us more than normal. But for the last few days, he's been staying away from you, too." He looked a bit smug. "If something was wrong between you two, he'd have been back with us. That means there is only something wrong with him."

"At least, wronger than normal," John clarified.

"Oh." Jan blinked. "You guys are really close, aren't you?"

The three of us nodded. I returned to looking out the window.

"Probably know each other way too well, don't you?" she asked.

Without looking at any of them, I declared, "It depends. Sometimes it's good to be with people who know you so well you don't have to finish sentences, people you can count on for anything."

"So, Daniels," John stated. "What are you getting us into?"

I looked at each of them, John last. "I know you never listen to the news, and if your parents heard, they're probably trying to protect you, so I'm going to tell you. Martin Franklin escaped," I revealed. "He's been following me. I've tried to keep him away from you guys until the police catch him, but I think it's going to be up to us to do something about him."

I proceeded to tell them about the last three days.

CHAPTER FORTY

I called Hanley. "What do you want, Daniels?"

I thought he'd have been happier to hear from me.

"We need to work together to get Franklin," I told him.

"No. We don't," Hanley retorted. "If you have any ideas or clues or other information that will allow us to capture him, you need to share it. Then you need to let us do our jobs and stay out of the way."

"It's not that simple," I insisted. "He's been following me. Every day after school. I can feel him. I lead him to Latisha Ford's house and watch for him. But I never see him. Then I wait until dark and sneak home. Like that first day when you told me about his escape. I know he's there. I can feel him. And we need to fix this."

"I'm going to hate myself. Linda is going to want to kill me, and I can only imagine what your mom will do to me," Hanley grumbled. "But...what are you suggesting?"

"Use me for bait."

"Out of the question."

"I think there's a way we can do it safely."

CHAPTER FORTY-ONE

I was walking down a long hallway. It reminded me of the one in the Thompsons' house except it didn't have any doors, and it didn't end. A corner was in sight but still a long way off.

Light came from nowhere. It didn't provide illumination, only shadows. My footsteps were not audible. Neither were the footsteps of the three following me. Jan was close, hanging onto the tail of my shirt. Warren was behind her, then John.

We were so close together it was tough taking real steps.

"We need to hurry," John urged. He looked over his shoulder, then released a deep, shaky breath.

"Yeah, we do," Warren agreed. "Something is coming."

Whatever was back there did not make any noise and was not visible. Yet I felt pressure, like it was pushing the air before itself as it came our way.

I shoved Jan, Warren, and John ahead of me. "Go. Run."

Warren and John did not have to be told a second time. They took off at a sprint, with Warren leading the way.

Jan continued to pull at my shirt. "C'mon."

"I'm coming," I told her. "You need to go ahead. Don't wait for me."

"You'd never leave me. I'm not leaving you." My shirt was about to tear where her fingers clenched at the hem.

I looked down the hallway. The pressure still followed, but the shadows faded into darkness not far from where we were. "You're not leaving me. I'm right behind you, but you need to hurry. Please run now."

She let go of my shirt and started to trot. I ran fast enough for her to know I was coming and that she should accelerate, which she did. I looked ahead. Warren and John had reached the corner and made the turn. "Catch up to them," I insisted. "We'll be fine."

Jan and I slid around the corner. We entered the hallway leading to Latisha Ford's bedroom and continued to run. A door stood at the end, barely visible in the shadows. Warren and John were nowhere to be seen. "Keep going," I told Jan. "Don't stop."

We fast approached the door. "Don't slow down. Barrel right through." Our hands hit the door together, and it parted in the middle and let us out of the hallway.

Our momentum carried us a few steps down a garden path. We looked at each other over a hedge. The hedge creaked and bent and closed in behind us, so we moved forward. I lost sight of Jan as the hedge continued to grow taller and leaned in my direction.

"Jan?" I called. Nothing came back.

A few seconds later, I heard, "Daniels, are you there?"

I yelled back.

"Daniels, where did you go? Did you leave me?"

I yelled again.

"Daniels, why won't you talk to me? Where are you? What did you do?" The last three questions were progressively quieter as if she was moving away.

I tried to force my way through the hedge. The branches swatted at me, scratched my face, and pulled at my clothes. When I stepped back and took a run at it, the hedge flung me back. Time seemed to stop as I floated through the air.

A faint light shined beneath the door into my bedroom. I lay still and let my eyes move around. All seemed as it should.

A weight settled on the corner of my bed. I rolled onto my side and looked at Great Grandma Nan. She stared into the growing darkness in the corner of my room. Movement flickered, and Rachel Thompson eased to the edge of the shadow.

"I lost them, didn't I?" I asked. "I lost them all."

"Only in that dream," Great Grandma Nan assured me. "Nothing is lost forever."

"But I can still screw this up, can't I?"

"Yes."

"I'm afraid I will. I'm not ready for this kind of thing."

"Sometimes, we have no choice," Great Grandma Nan pronounced.

Rachel stepped forward, out of the shadow. She wore

the dress I had last seen her in. The one she wore to her cremation. The corners of her mouth lifted in an almost-smile. A tear rolled down her cheek. She was still lovely. My hand lifted toward her, then fell back to the bed before she noticed.

"Today is the day," Great Grandma Nan stated. "But you already knew that."

"Yeah, I did."

"Be careful you don't lose yourself, too." Great Grandma Nan rose from my bed and walked into the shadow, where Rachel had already disappeared.

My whole body twitched, and I was awake, sitting up in bed.

CHAPTER FORTY-TWO

John and Warren skipped school. They had one errand to attend to, then they were supposed to stay locked in the house. In order for my plan to work, I needed to know they were safely hidden away. Warren didn't mind. He almost never missed school, even when he was sick, but he had a Social Studies exam he hadn't bothered to study for. Staying away bought him some more time. John had reservations, however, and they had nothing to do with school.

Hanley and Morse, wearing jeans, sweatshirts, and light jackets, came into school at the beginning of last hour and pulled Jan and me from our classes. Jan was their cover. They were to escort her from school, hopefully looking like her parents taking her to an appointment.

In reality, they'd come to put a microphone, transmitter, and receiver on me. I would go through my usual routine. Walk home from school by myself and end up at Latisha Ford's house. After I was wired and we'd run a test, the three of them left. I waited until the final bell for the day and set out.

Maybe it was the excitement, the anticipation of doing something important, the nightmares and visits from Great Grandma Nan and Rachel, or I was too caught up in my plan. Whatever it was, I managed to overlook the fact that things felt different from all the other days since Franklin's escape. The differences grew in intensity the closer I got to the Fords' house until they reached the point where they could not be ignored.

The microphone and receiver were short-range, but that shouldn't have been a problem. Hanley and Morse would arrive at the house about the same time I did.

Then it dawned on me why it felt different. Things were not going according to my plan. For one, I must have walked quicker, more directly than I had the other days, because I made good time getting there.

I stood at the bus stop for a while and watched the house. It had been part of my routine most of the days Franklin followed me, but this time I stood there at least twice as long as I had previously. Still no signal from Hanley and Morse indicating they were in the neighborhood, within radio range, and ready to move as soon as I suggested Franklin was there.

I continued to watch the house. Nothing moved, either living or dead. I kept babbling into the microphone, hoping they would suddenly be in range and answer. The conversation remained one-sided. I felt my paranoia increase like it was ascending some kind of meter or scale. Every few minutes, it spiked higher, like the temperature as the sun climbed in the afternoon.

My nerves tingled, my paranoia screamed, and I started wondering if I should head in the opposite direction when

I heard a whisper. "Daniels? Are you there?" It was Morse. "We should be in range. Where are you?"

I sighed in relief, though my spine was jelly. "It's good to hear from you. I'm at the bus stop. Something is wrong, though."

"Why? What's up? Have you seen something?"

"No, nothing. But the feelings have changed."

Hanley came on. "We need more than that. What else can you tell us?"

"Nothing."

"What do you want to do?" Hanley requested.

I hesitated for a breath, then another. "Keep to the plan."

"Daniels, don't be foolish," Morse insisted. "This is risky. If things aren't going according to plan already, we should drop it. We may not be able to protect you."

"How long until you're here?" I asked.

"We're about three minutes out," Hanley remarked.

"I'm going into the house," I declared. "No matter what happens, make sure you get him." I started across the street, headed for the front sidewalk.

"You need to wait," Morse told me.

"We need to improvise, resort to other contingencies. Something." I was at the door. "I'm going in."

Morse almost yelled, "What contingencies? You shouldn't even know that word. Daniels, what are you up to?"

"Switching to radio silence. At least from this end. See you soon."

I opened the unlocked front door and entered the house. It was silent.

Some profanity from Morse tickled my ear, then the radio went silent from their end, too.

I crossed the living room and headed toward the stairs. No signs of ghosts, no visions, no cold spots. No noises, no funny feelings. A couple of dust bunnies swirled, but I considered them harmless. Too much traffic had flowed through the house. The footprints in the thin coating of dust on the wood floors, most of them mine, had become indistinguishable.

No sign of Martin Franklin.

I crept up the stairs and made my way into Latisha's bedroom. I looked out the window and saw Hanley and Morse pull around the house in an unmarked car, headed toward the alley. Hanley whispered, "Daniels, should we come in?"

"No. Not yet."

"Who ya talkin' to?" somebody behind me asked.

CHAPTER FORTY-THREE

I turned and faced Martin Franklin, who stood in the doorway to Latisha's bedroom. He was tall and thin and wore a Hennepin County Sheriff's Deputy uniform. It didn't fit well. It was long enough but still too large for him. I locked my gaze on his. "John Thompson," I told him. "You remember John. You murdered his sister."

His eyes narrowed for a fraction of a second.

"John is a technology nut. He bought miniature short-range radios, like walkie-talkies. I got this ear thing." I tapped the receiver in my ear. "And a tiny microphone in my shirt." I patted my tee shirt so he could see where it was. "We're trying them out while we explore this haunted house."

"No such thing."

"Sure there is." I smiled at him. John had actually given me another piece of technology, just in case. I had a miniature digital recorder in my pocket. It was set to begin recording by pressing one button. I reached into my pants pocket, then found and depressed the record button.

A.W. POWERS

"You don't know this house, do you?" I asked.

"It's your house," he claimed. "You come here every day."

I shook my head. "I knew you were following me. I've been leading you here."

"Bullshit. You never saw me. You never knew I was there."

"I've known it since the day you escaped," I stated. "And I've been setting you up. Someone here wants to meet you."

"Bullshit. Ain't nobody here."

"Latisha Ford lives here," I countered. "You must remember her. You murdered her, too."

His eyes narrowed again.

I had a sad realization and shook my head. "It's not that you don't remember your victims. It's that you don't even know who they are, do you? You have no idea who you kill. They're only a thing you use. You don't know them before, and you don't know them when you're done. Knowing their names would make it too personal. I'm guessing you only know the name of my friend Rachel Thompson because you had to sit through your trial, and she was the only one they talked about. You don't even ask who they are, do you?" I glared at him. "Other than enjoying the kill, you don't care."

His eyes appeared the way I remembered the first time I saw them. Dark and cold. "I know you," he intoned. "I'm going to enjoy killing you." He took another step into the room and pushed the door shut. I heard wood meet wood, but I didn't hear the latch click. "When your momma comes home, I'm gonna kill her. She's not my type, kind of old, but she's still a fine piece of ass. I can enjoy doing that."

I shook my head. "No. You won't be anywhere near my mom."

"Then I'm gonna find that little girlfriend of yours," Franklin continued. "The one with the crazy hair. She's exactly my type."

I smiled at him. "You're not going to kill anyone. You're not getting out of here. It's over. Is there anyone you want to call to come kiss your posterior goodbye?"

In my ear, I heard Hanley say, "Daniels, we're on our way in. Don't do anything crazy."

The picture of Latisha on the dresser, the one I had borrowed and returned, rotated until it faced Franklin. I saw it moving from the corner of my eye. I knew Franklin saw it because his eyes got huge.

The closet door swung shut. I wanted to laugh. I knew who was in control. Then all the doors throughout the house slammed shut just as Hanley hit the front door.

In stereo, in my ear and from outside the house, I heard Hanley shout, "Latisha, let us in." He slammed against the door again. It didn't budge. Hanley and Morse were outside, and I was trapped in the bedroom with a serial killer and a pissed-off ghost.

I inched toward Latisha's bed. Franklin stepped toward the center of the room and pulled an ivory and metal handle from his pocket. He depressed a button, and a six-inch blade snapped into place.

"I brought this for you," he offered.

"No, actually, you didn't," I rebuked. "You hid it some-where and somehow got it back since you escaped. You take it everywhere with you. It's how you control your victims. You threaten their families, tell them you're going to use that knife on all of them if they give you any trouble."

"Gee. You're pretty smart for a young punk."

I shrugged. "I know things."

"Knowing things don't help you when you're dead." He stepped forward.

The closet door flew open and slammed against the wall hard enough to embed the doorknob in the plaster. Latisha's yearbook shot out from the stack on the shelf and hit Franklin in the temple. Too late, his arms came up and covered his head. The switchblade fell to the floor with a solid *thunk* as it stuck point-first.

"I told you it was over. I told you someone was waiting for you. And Latisha is pissed." I put my hands on my temples and closed my eyes like I was concentrating. "I'm getting a message." I snapped my eyes open wide and looked at him. My hands remained at my temples. "She's not alone. She says you believe in ghosts. She says you believe in haunted houses. You know they're real. She says all of your victims are here. They've been waiting for you. All of them, every single girl you've killed."

"You don't hear nothin'," Franklin yelled. "There are no ghosts."

"Latisha says it's time for you to die."

He backed toward the door as the picture lifted off the dresser, the yearbook raised from the floor, and more books flew out of the closet. They spun in a circle in the middle of the room.

Franklin pulled a gun from behind his back. It must have been the one he took from the deputy he killed.

It was ripped from his fingers and flew into the closet.

The sound of Hanley slamming against the back door was joined by someone, probably Morse, crashing into the front door.

Franklin's switchblade began to vibrate, then pulled from the floor and joined the other things circling the room.

His fear must have made him forget he intended to kill me. He turned, grabbed the doorknob, and pulled. The door wouldn't open. With both hands on the knob, he pulled and bounced.

The yearbook left the torrent and hit him in the shoulder. He turned and saw the switchblade streaking toward his face, gleaming, evil-point-first. Franklin ducked to the side. The blade went past his cheek and stuck in the door. A fine line of blood welled along a nick in his earlobe.

The switchblade wouldn't budge when he jerked at it. He pounded on the door with a large fist, then pulled again with both hands and a foot against the doorframe. It reminded me of a cartoon.

Latisha must have let go of the door because it opened. Franklin fell backward but caught himself before he fell. He was through the door in a heartbeat and headed down the hallway.

As he thundered down the stairs, I announced into the microphone, "Franklin's coming out. Be ready."

I scrambled for the bed. The errand John and Warren had completed earlier in the day while they were supposed to be at school was part of my contingency plan. It had brought them here.

Warren came from a family of hunters. On my behalf, he told his dad I wanted to borrow a shotgun to take a gun safety course and that my mom had approved. Mr. Marsh had readily agreed. The plan, as presented to Mr. Marsh, involved Warren dropping the gun off at my house on his way to school. Instead, Warren and John had brought it to Latisha's room and stashed it under her bed.

One way or another, Martin Franklin's reign of terror would end this day.

Considering how my plan hadn't worked very well, I hoped Latisha was on our side. I hoped she'd recognized John and let him and Warren into the house and that they were gone before Franklin decided to let himself in. If not, I had put them in harm's way. That misstep in my plan would have been tragic.

Then I wondered if Franklin had to work to get into the house or if Latisha had her own plan and let him in the same as she did me every day when I came over.

I reached under the bed. No shotgun. I groped further. Still no shotgun. That meant he'd been here when my friends arrived, and I'd probably gotten them killed. There would be no forgiving myself if that were true.

I dropped to the floor. "Please, God, don't do this." I knelt and looked under the bed.

The shotgun waited for me close to the wall.

I breathed a sigh of relief. That meant Latisha had let them in and they were probably okay, hiding safely. I had to believe Franklin hadn't seen them.

The shotgun was an old .410-gauge double barrel, which Warren had hopefully loaded with birdshot. I grabbed the weapon and got to my feet. I moved to the windows, where I had a view of the side and front yards, and tried to see where Franklin would exit the house.

He chose the front door.

CHAPTER FORTY-FOUR

Hoping for a shot, I opened the bedroom window in time to see Franklin and Morse fly off the steps. Their limbs tangled as they wrestled for her gun. I knew I didn't have a shot, so I shouted into the microphone, "Hanley, he's out front, fighting with Morse."

Hanley whipped around the corner of the house just as Franklin scrambled away from Morse. Franklin jumped to his feet with Morse's gun in his right hand.

Hanley had his pistol up and pointed at Franklin. "Franklin! Minneapolis Police! Drop the weapon!"

Morse was still on the ground.

I aimed the shotgun at Franklin. Morse was too close. I might hit her with birdshot. If only he'd take a few steps farther away...

Franklin stared at the front porch, wide-eyed, not paying attention to any of us. "No," he stated. "Can't be." I wish I could have seen what he saw.

I kept the shotgun pointed at Franklin but also tried to keep an eye on Morse. I needed to know where she was and if she was in any danger. Or from me. I saw her slowly reach toward her ankle, where she pulled a small pistol.

Hanley shouted again. This time, Franklin seemed to hear him. Franklin turned and glanced at Hanley, then brought the gun around.

Hanley fired. Morse fired. Hanley fired again.

All three bullets hit Franklin and knocked him to the ground.

I turned and ran from the bedroom. By the time I went through the front door, Hanley had picked up Morse's gun and was checking Franklin for a pulse. I stood there, staring at Franklin, the shotgun pointed at his face. His dark eyes open but blank, the glare of evil gone. Blood oozed from beneath him and from the three holes in his chest.

Hanley went to Morse. She was in the process of standing, but he grabbed her and almost lifted her off the ground as he pulled her into a hug. She hugged him back.

"You had me scared there for a minute," Hanley declared.

"Me, too," Morse stated. "We can talk about it later. I'm okay."

"Good. I'm glad."

"I'm glad, too," I remarked. "But I still have to ask. Just how close friends are you two?"

Hanley let go of Morse and pointed at the shotgun. "What were you going to do with that?"

"One of my contingencies. Keeping our options open," I told him. "I knew this would end today, one way or another. You should always have contingency plans ready. Even for your contingency plans."

"Is it loaded?" he asked.

"Of course. Otherwise, there wasn't much point in aiming at him."

"Hand it over." He held out a hand and wiggled his fingers.

I pressed the thumb lever and opened the barrels, extracted the two shells, and handed the gun to Hanley, still broken. "Be careful. It's not mine." He wiggled his fingers again, and I passed him the shells, which he dropped into his pocket.

"Was Latisha there? In the bedroom?" Hanley asked. The shotgun rested on his shoulder.

"Yeah."

"Did you actually get a message from her?" Morse asked.

"No." I shrugged and smiled. "I figured the way he denied the existence of ghosts and haunted houses, he might actually believe in them. I made the message up."

Morse smiled and shook her head. "Nice piece of improv."

Hanley made a sound that may have been a chuckle.

At least one of the neighbors called the police about the shooting. While Morse called it in on the car radio, Hanley stowed the shotgun in the trunk.

Within minutes, the place was crawling with police. Morse and Hanley's superior officers pulled them aside and turned them over to Internal Affairs, who in turn called the Hennepin County Sheriff's office to objectively handle the investigation. Having lost one of their own to the dead man, the sheriffs handed it over to the Bureau of Criminal Apprehension.

Hennepin County District Attorney Harry Schmidt, along with a couple of high-ranking cops, gloated for the media at the street corner. Schmidt exclaimed his pride in the way his people handled themselves and the investigation and how they'd eliminated the evil serial killer. He didn't say anything about the escape. I shook my head. He was oblivious to what had really happened but knew enough to take credit for it.

Everyone seemed able to overlook my presence and the fact that I was involved. Or that I had recorded portions of the exchange. After all, I was a civilian and a juvenile. They did "borrow" John's recorder, though.

The people handling the investigation let Hanley and Morse go after a few hours. By then, Martin Franklin had been hauled away, and the crime scene investigators had been through the house. Schmidt and most of the high-ranking cops had wandered off, but the media still lurked, hoping for something they could use to lead the nightly news.

When Hanley, Morse, and I got to my house, I called Jan. She answered on the first ring, "Daniels?"

"Yeah, it's me."

"Thank God. Are you okay?"

"Fine," I told her. "It's over."

"That's a relief."

"How did you know it was me calling?" I asked.

"Wishful thinking, I guess," Jan admitted. "I've probably

called John and Warren by your name a couple of times without knowing it."

"You've talked to the guys?"

"A bunch of times. John called every few minutes, it seemed. In between, Warren called. He said he was making sure I was okay."

"Uh-huh. That's just like him. So, you three are okay?" I asked. "I can quit worrying?"

"Yeah, we're all fine. We were wondering what was happening, going nuts, worried to death about you, but we're fine."

"Well, it's over. The police got him." I heard her sigh. "Will you call the guys and come over? I'll tell the three of you about it."

Morse and Hanley told my mom about our little adventure. She listened quietly. I stood next to her. She kept her hand on me. It would occasionally drift up to my neck as if she wanted to wring it.

Hanley concluded with, "He's fast-thinking and brave, quite resourceful. He needs to be careful, especially about dragging his friends into things. Keep him on a short leash."

Morse gave me a hug. "I don't want to see you again until you graduate. Except maybe at a competition or a holiday. Something good. Stay out of trouble and take care of your mom."

They walked out as Jan, John, and Warren arrived. Hanley offered them an actual smile. Morse called, "See you, kids. Take care." And they were gone.

I spent the evening telling Jan, Warren, and John about Latisha and Martin Franklin. We sat in the living room, and Mom hung out in the kitchen. Every once in a while, she'd come to the doorway and listen. She didn't look happy, but she didn't look disapproving, either. I tried not to sound too excited about the whole thing, but sometimes I got carried away. Especially about Latisha and the doors and the flying yearbook and switchblade.

I didn't tell them Franklin threatened Mom and Jan. He couldn't do anything about it now, so they didn't need to know.

John, the wannabe parapsychologist, proclaimed, "I wish I could have seen everything she did. I am bummed. You did turn on the recorder, right?"

"I did, but I don't know if it caught anything you'll be able to hear. Or if the police will give it back," I mentioned.

"You let the police steal my recorder?"

"I didn't let them," I insisted. "I didn't have any choice."

"Well, I have something you haven't seen yet," he declared. "When Warren and I left Latisha's room, I opened the curtains. When we got down to the street, I turned and took a picture. You know, in case you destroyed the place or it imploded around you."

"You mean, in case it got sucked to hell and took me along."

"Exactly," John agreed. "Anyway, look at this." He held out his camera for me to see.

In the center of the picture was Latisha's bedroom. In the window was Latisha Ford.

"You need to find a way to make sure that never disappears," I stated. "You have your first evidence of something."

"I do, don't I?"

"I'll write down what happened, just in case," I promised. "Either way, Martin Franklin is done."

Like I didn't tell them about the threats, I didn't tell him how different things could have ended if it hadn't been for Latisha and all the paranormal events.

The next day, we all went to Latisha Ford's home after school. We ducked under the crime scene tape, went upstairs, and sat in her bedroom, talking about nothing and everything. I pointed out where the switchblade had stuck in the floor and later in the door. It was gone, so the police lab guys must have pulled it free. We all stood around the door and examined Franklin's footprint where he had planted it on the frame as he struggled with the unlocked door that wouldn't open. We picked up the yearbook and other things that had landed on the floor, and we returned them to where we thought they belonged.

John turned ghastly white, and Jan yelped when we heard the door open downstairs. Warren and I merely stiffened. All of us flinched as a cat ran into the room and jumped on the bed. It was the cat from the pictures. We relaxed when we heard voices and knew the door had been opened by the living.

We tried not to look guilty when Hanley, Morse, and a sad-looking woman with a girl a few years older than us found us.

Hanley seemed to look only at me. "Breaking and entering?" he asked. "And into a sealed crime scene?"

"These are the kids we were telling you about," Morse announced. "The ones who helped us find Latisha's killer."

Introductions were made all around. Hanley and Morse had tracked down Latisha's mom and sister and brought them home. When we found out who they were, we quickly expressed our condolences for her daughter and husband, even though they were somewhat late. Mrs. Ford, in turn, expressed her condolences to John for Rachel, who choked out a quiet "Thank you."

When she told him, "If you or your folks need anything, you come see me," he almost managed a smile and a nod.

Then she looked at me. "I understand because of you, two more daughters have been found. Two more mothers can rest a little easier."

I glanced at Morse. She explained, "Yesterday, while we were taking care of you-know-what, the lab guys found two more girls in the cemetery. Things are beginning to pick up some momentum. Evidently, it's too big for us now. The feds are coming to help."

Mrs. Ford looked around the room, then wrapped an arm around her daughter's shoulders. Which was difficult since her daughter was taller than her. "Things are different than when we left," she remarked. "Do you feel it, LaNaya?"

Latisha's sister nodded and smiled.

"It feels peaceful now. Before, it felt angry. We couldn't be here. We had to leave." She smiled at LaNaya. "I think we can come home now. I think your sister is at peace." Then she looked at John and added, "Yours, too."

I hoped she was correct.

Two days later, on Sunday evening, John appeared at my door. He held up his recorder. "Officer Hanley dropped it off. He doesn't think anybody actually listened to it," he told me. "So I did."

"Did it work?" I asked.

"Yeah. It worked great."

"Did it tell you anything I didn't already tell you?"

His brow lifted. "Depends."

"Depends on what?"

"Did you hear voices?" he asked me. "Did Latisha speak?"

"No. What's going on?"

"After I listened to the tape…oh, about twelve times, I started doing a little research. And I learned about EVPs."

"Cool. It's about time," I remarked. "What are EVPs?"

"Electronic voice phenomenon," John revealed. "Apparently, spirits speak on recordings when they can't be heard in person."

"Also cool. So?"

"So, my recorder contains some EVPs," he explained. "You picked up the voice of a spirit while you were talking with Martin Franklin, the murderous bastard."

"Is that an official title?" I inquired. "Did somebody pronounce it? Like on the tape or in the paper or something?"

"No. Just me."

"You heard somebody besides me, him, Morse, and Hanley on the recording?"

"Yeah."

"I think we better listen to it," I declared.

I plopped onto the couch. John sat on the edge of the cushion, pressed a button, and set the recorder on the coffee table. He began to rock, one foot tapping.

The recording hissed, then I listened to my conversation with Martin Franklin. I didn't like my voice. It didn't sound like me. About the time I told him I was getting a message, a chorus of voices joined us. They chanted, "No more." From the differences in tone and volume, it sounded as if it was coming from all around me. "It ends" began to mix into the chant.

John reached out and paused the playback. "You look like a codfish."

"What?" I asked.

"From Mary Poppins. She tells Michael to close his mouth, he looks like a codfish," John quipped. "That's how you look. Your mouth is hanging open, and you're all white. So I guess you look a little like a dead codfish."

"Thanks," I intoned. "And thank you for not taking my picture."

"You're welcome." He reached for the recorder.

"Did that sound like one voice? Or did it sound like more than one person?"

"I was hoping you'd say something about that. I thought it sounded like a bunch of people. All female, but definitely more than one."

"Yeah," I agreed. "So I didn't lie to him. Latisha wasn't alone."

"Evidently not," John stated. "Do you feel better knowing you didn't lie to a mass murderer about multiple ghosts coming for him?"

"Yeah...well, no. I guess I don't care," I remarked. "Or at least I shouldn't. He's still a worse person."

"Exactly." John pressed play, and the recording continued.

After Hanley yelled at Franklin on the tape, a voice intoned, "Time to die."

"That was only one person," John pointed out.

"I think it was the first one to speak earlier," I suggested. "I wonder if that was Latisha."

We heard the gunshots, followed by "Goodbye." There was a pause, then someone announced, "I'm ready, Daddy. We can go now."

I stared at the recorder. "Wow."

John turned off the machine. "Do we dare play this for someone so we can find out if it was her?" he asked.

"I don't think we dare," I told him. "Not for a while. The only people we know who'd recognize her voice are her family, and that wouldn't be right."

"I suppose not," John conceded. "They knew she was there, though."

"They did, and they could tell she was gone when they came back. But I don't know that they'd want their final memory of Latisha to be a vengeful ghost. That isn't how I'd want to be remembered."

"I can see you as the spirit of revenge," John suggested. "Or maybe justice. I think you'll get most of it before you die."

"You think so?" I asked.

"Yeah. Just a funny feeling."

"Those are supposed to be mine. And I hate them," I admitted. "They're never really funny."

THE STORY CONTINUES

The The Psychic Guardian Ange story continues with
book two, *No Rest for the Dead.*

Claim your copy today!

AUTHOR NOTES - A.W. POWERS

FEB 17, 2023

"I know where you live."

I don't actually, but it used to be an effective threat. Until everybody used it and it quit being a threat.

I used to say, "If I want to find you bad enough, there is nowhere you can hide," because I was psychic and knew things.

Then I let Jacob Daniels use the line. I became less psychic and knew fewer things.

I believe everyone has some psychic ability. Most of us don't realize it, don't know that what we use every day is some type of extrasensory perception. We couldn't control it if we knew we had it, or we deny its existence so no one thinks we're a fruitcake.

We're all fruitcakes in some manner. Uniquely so. And it's amazing.

My aunt Sis told me about the time her parents and husband came to visit her from beyond the grave. She believed it was real.

Another time, my aunt Susie told me Sis's story. Susie believed as well.

When my cousin called to tell me Susie had died, I stayed awake the rest of the night, waiting to see if she might come visit me. I believed. She didn't visit. Her not coming did not prove anything. I still believed.

Do you believe?

Does your family have ghost stories, too?

Jacob Daniels was born out of my nightmares. They are frequently violent, and they leave me rattled, frustrated, and far from rested. They will repeat if I ignore them. The first nightmare that contributed to my writing was so bad, I woke up shaking.

The first book I wrote, which is not the novel you are reading here but is waiting for its time, used three of my nightmares. The one that left me shaking, I used in its entirety.

For a long time, I didn't bother to watch horror movies. They were never as scary as my nightmares. I should probably try again. Maybe answer a few questions. Have movies gotten scarier, or have I become more sensitive and able to be frightened, or have I grown immune to imagined fears, or have my fear receptors been overwhelmed by real life?

So many questions.

The question that fed *First Casualty* is, "How many people go missing every year?"

The statistics are frightening. I'm not going to include them here. If you want to know what I've learned, come to an event and ask me. I'll be happy to tell you. Well...maybe not happy. As I said, the statistics are frightening. The truth behind them is dark, frustrating and even more frightening. I'm willing to discuss the subject because it's important. Just not happily.

There are many questions that need to be asked, many subjects that need to be discussed. One of the best aspects of writing is the ability to highlight and explore those subjects. But no subject, no story has only one side. Writing fiction allows me ask the questions and discuss both sides of any subject objectively. At least as objectively as any human is able.

Other writers, maybe all, explore those subjects too. They come at them from their perspective, flavored by their environment, education, history and their objectivity, just as I do. All those writers have something to share. As a result, I read to understand the world. But I write to understand me.

If only that were possible.

It's a journey.

Many people have helped me on this journey. Some of them without their knowledge or intent. Some by saying the correct thing at the best possible moment. I need to mention a few: my family, close and extended, the believers who indulged and encouraged me until this all became true. The Wordwhippers: Dale Butler, Barb Danson, Barbara Schmidt, Cathy Buchholz, Brittany Jaekel, Mary Rogers, Mary Sebesta, Liz Parker, and especially Joe and Denise Jubert. My continuity testers: Vicki Ryan and Carrie Johnson. And another early believer: Jeff Danielson. Thank you all.

To the rest of the world: you are my teachers, my inspiration and my hope. Keep it up. Hang in there. Stay hopeful. Thank you for joining me on this journey.

A.W. Powers
17-Feb-2023

Photo Note: Full saying on shirt: You're in my novel and it doesn't end well
Photo credit: Lauren R. Anderson

CONNECT WITH THE AUTHOR

Join A.W. Powers Email List here:

https://wmjanderson.com/a-w-powers/

Website:

https://wmjanderson.com/a-w-powers/

Facebook:

https://www.facebook.com/profile.php?id=
100088831614620

Amazon Author Page:

https://www.amazon.com/stores/A.W.-Powers/author/
B0C6FJGJQQ

BOOKS BY A.W. POWERS

The Psychic Guardian Angel

First Casualty (Book 1)

No Rest for the Dead (Book 2 - coming soon)

Flying Objects (Book 3 - coming soon)

Made in the USA
Monee, IL
09 August 2024

62973284R00177